THE MYSTICAL PENCIL

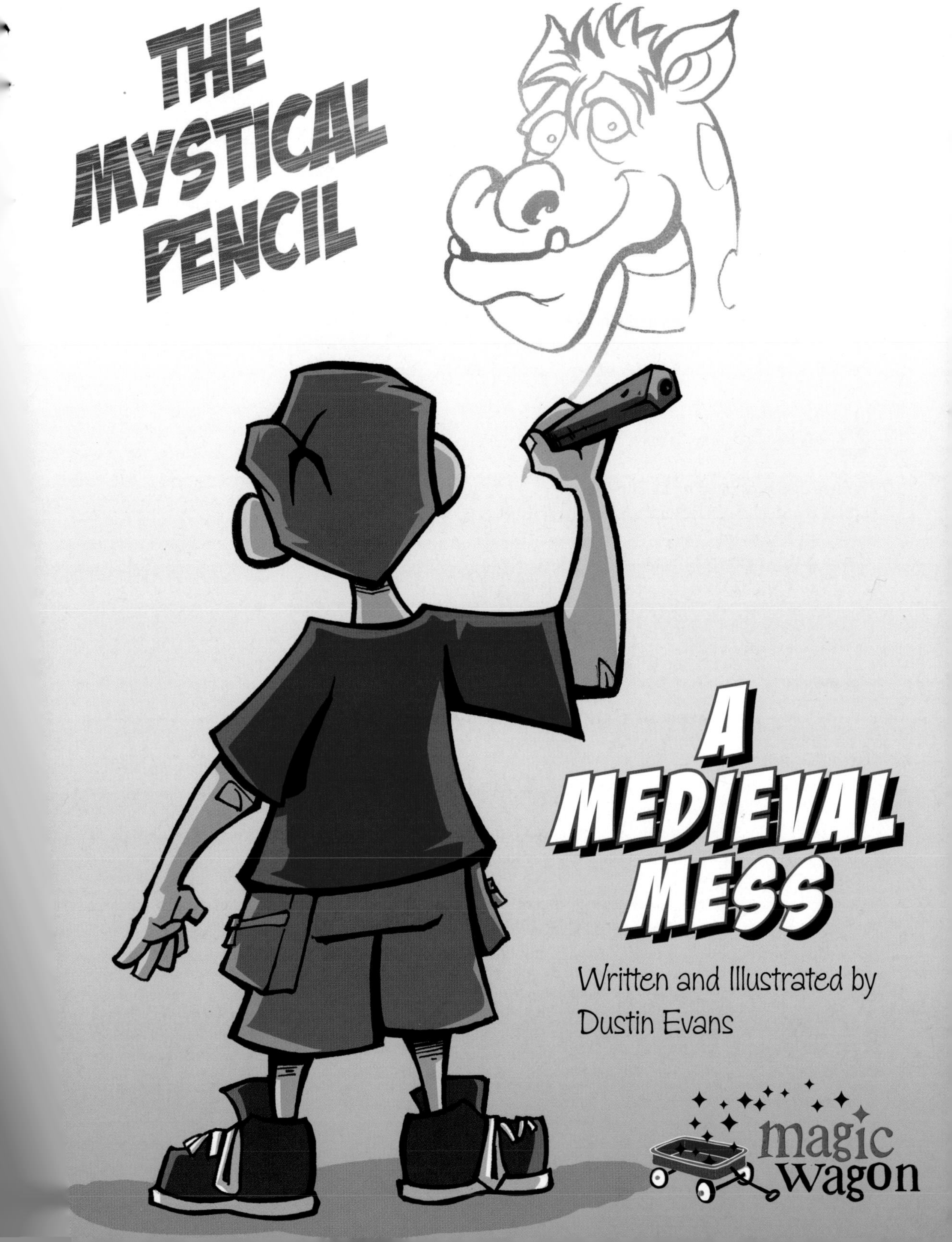

A MEDIEVAL MESS

Written and Illustrated by
Dustin Evans

magic wagon

visit us at
www.abdopublishing.com

Published by Magic Wagon, a division of the ABDO Group, PO Box 398166, Minneapolis, MN 55439. Copyright © 2013 by Abdo Consulting Group, Inc. International copyrights reserved in all countries. All rights reserved. No part of this book may be reproduced in any form without written permission from the publisher.

Graphic Planet™ is a trademark and logo of Magic Wagon.

Printed in the United States of America, North Mankato, Minnesota.
102012
012013
This book contains at least 10% recycled materials.

Written and Illustrated by Dustin Evans
Edited by Stephanie Hedlund and Rochelle Baltzer
Cover art by Dustin Evans
Cover design by Neil Klinepier

Library of Congress Cataloging-in-Publication Data

Evans, Dustin, 1982-
  A medieval mess / written & illustrated by Dustin Evans.
      p. cm. -- (The mystical pencil)
  Summary: Alex finds a strange pencil in his father's bag, and when the monster he draws with it comes to life disaster follows at the Renaissance fair.
  ISBN 978-1-61641-928-8
1. Pencils--Comic books, strips, etc. 2. Pencils--Juvenile fiction. 3. Monsters--Comic books, strips, etc. 4. Monsters--Juvenile fiction. 5. Renaissance fairs--Comic books, strips, etc. 6. Renaissance fairs--Juvenile fiction. 7. Imagination--Comic books, strips, etc. 8. Imagination--Juvenile fiction. 9. Graphic novels. [1. Graphic novels. 2. Pencils--Fiction. 3. Monsters--Fiction. 4. Renaissance fairs--Fiction. 5. Imagination--Fiction.] I. Title.
  PZ7.7.E92Med 2013
  741.5'973--dc23
                                    2012027940

Contents

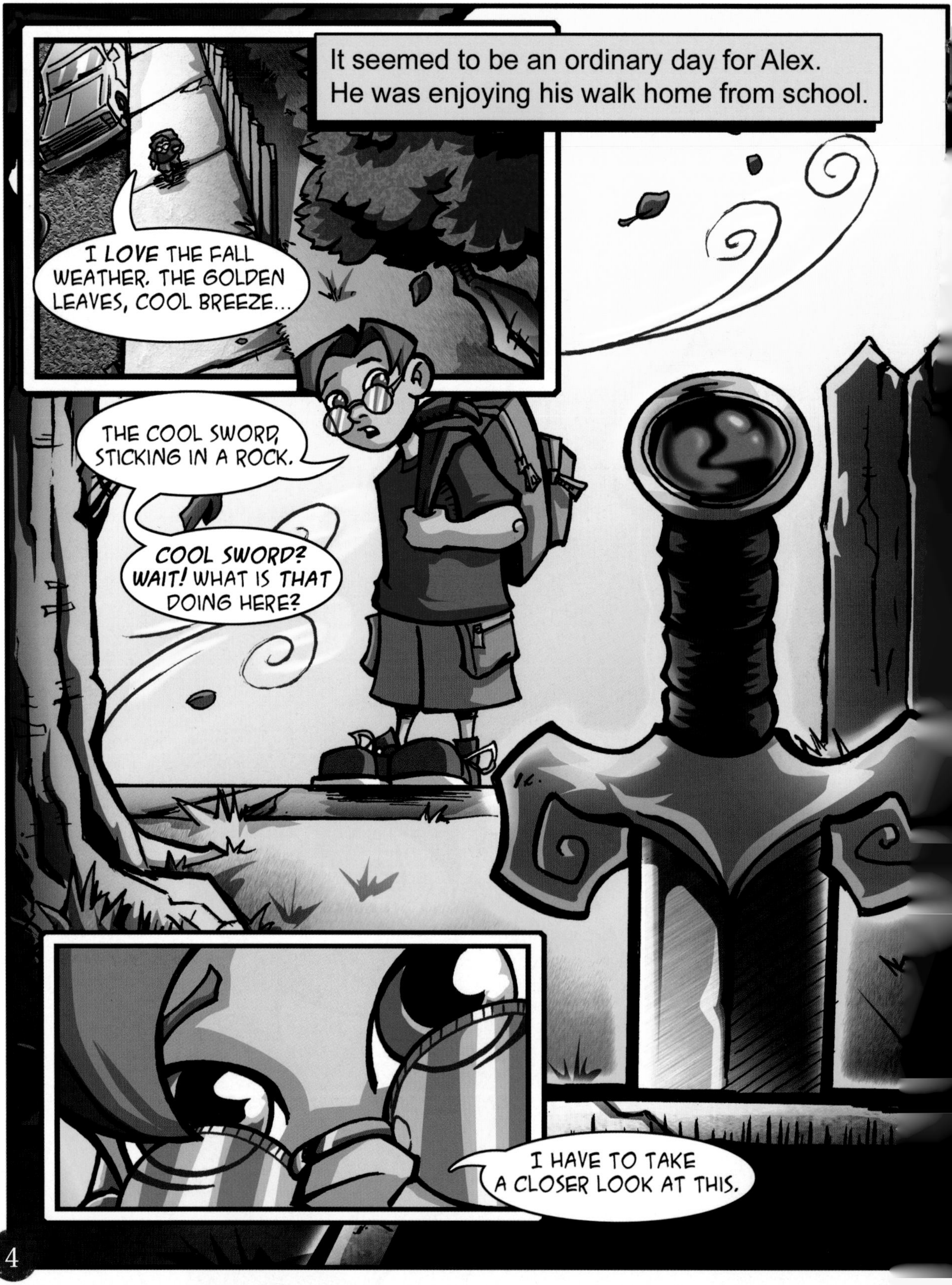
It seemed to be an ordinary day for Alex. He was enjoying his walk home from school.
I LOVE THE FALL WEATHER. THE GOLDEN LEAVES, COOL BREEZE...
THE COOL SWORD, STICKING IN A ROCK.
COOL SWORD? WAIT! WHAT IS THAT DOING HERE?
I HAVE TO TAKE A CLOSER LOOK AT THIS.

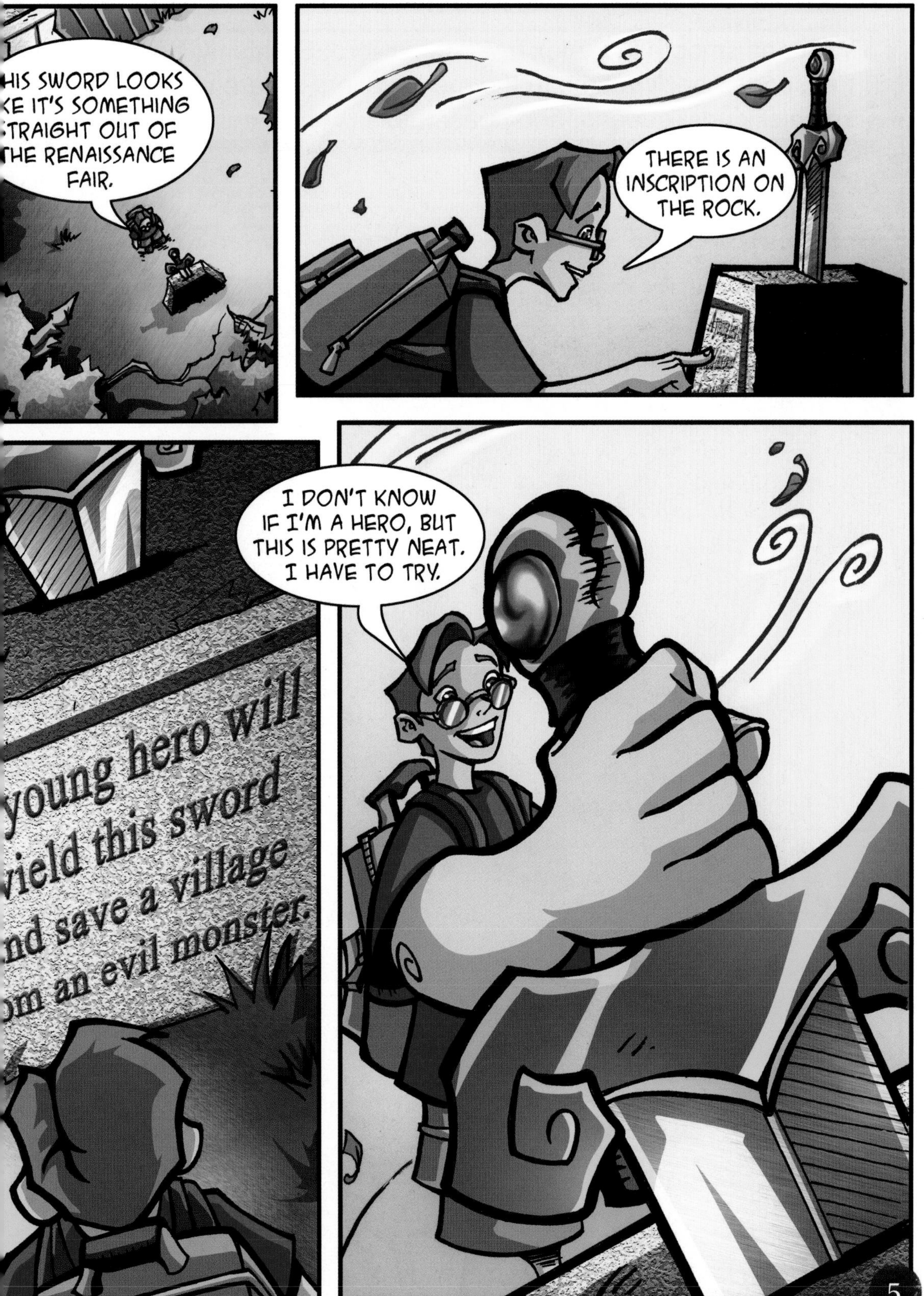
HIS SWORD LOOKS E IT'S SOMETHING TRAIGHT OUT OF THE RENAISSANCE FAIR.
THERE IS AN INSCRIPTION ON THE ROCK.
young hero will ield this sword nd save a village om an evil monster.
I DON'T KNOW IF I'M A HERO, BUT THIS IS PRETTY NEAT. I HAVE TO TRY.

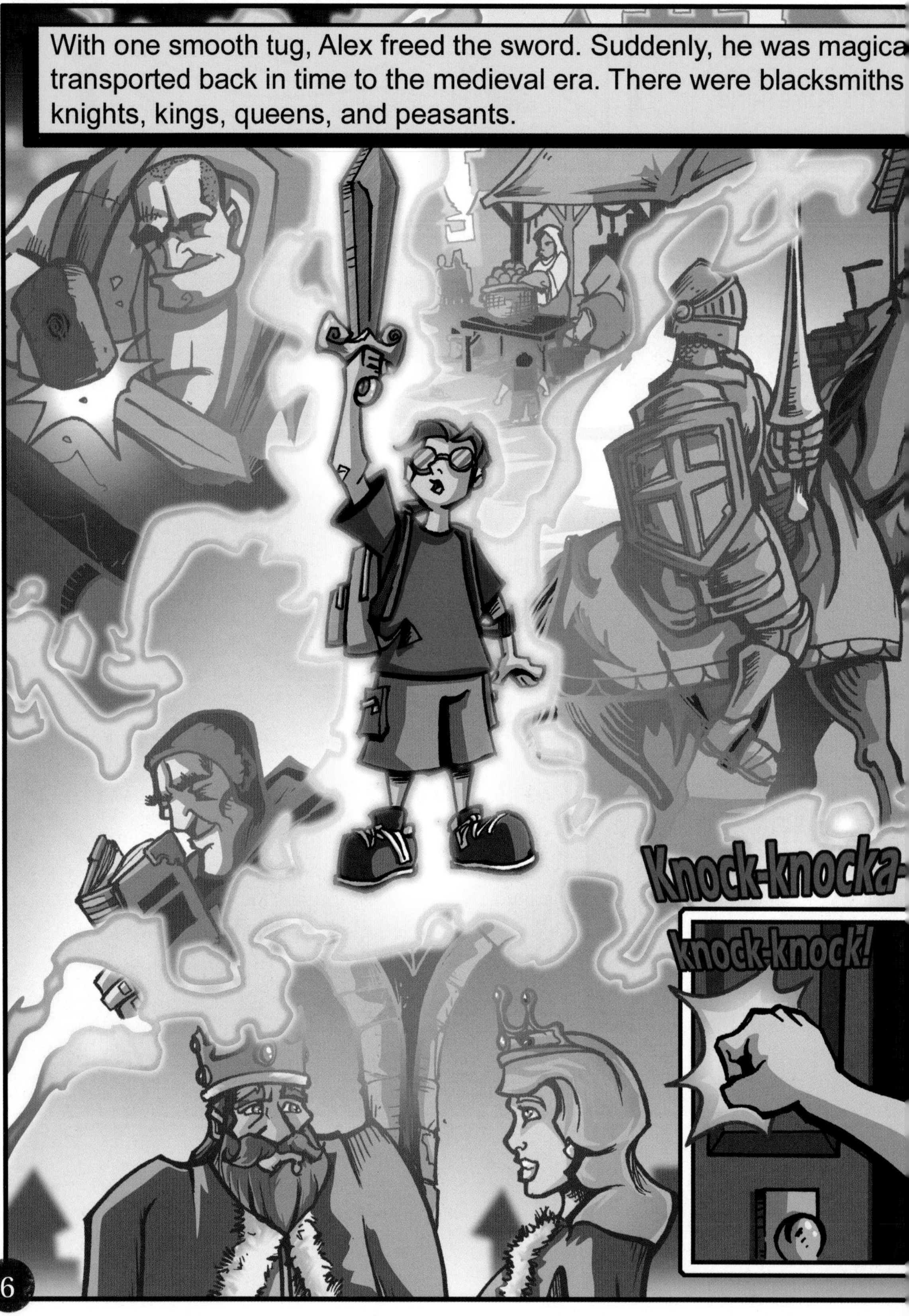
With one smooth tug, Alex freed the sword. Suddenly, he was magica
transported back in time to the medieval era. There were blacksmiths
knights, kings, queens, and peasants.
Knock-knocka-
knock-knock!

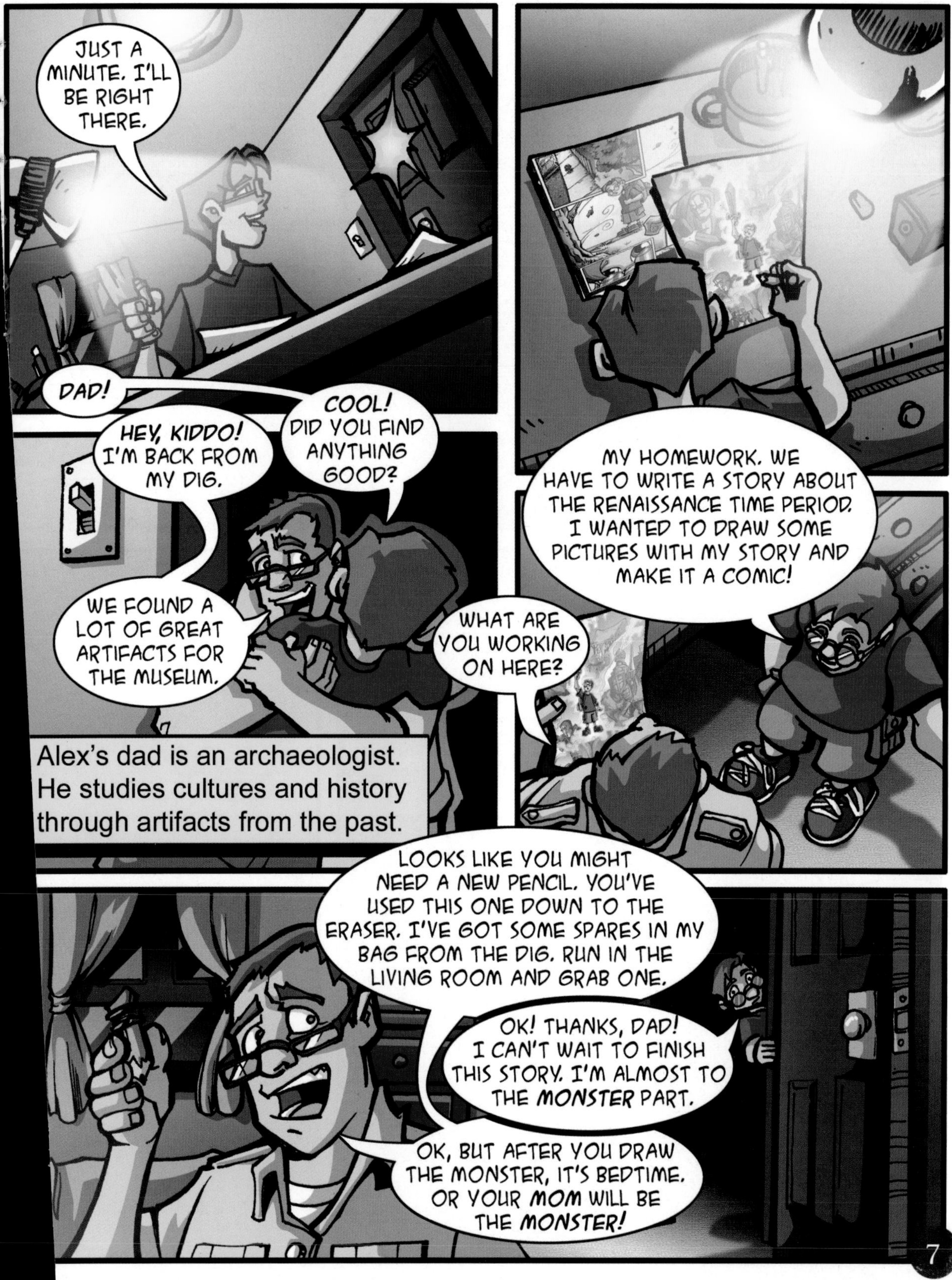
JUST A MINUTE. I'LL BE RIGHT THERE.
DAD!
COOL! DID YOU FIND ANYTHING GOOD?
HEY, KIDDO! I'M BACK FROM MY DIG.
WE FOUND A LOT OF GREAT ARTIFACTS FOR THE MUSEUM.
WHAT ARE YOU WORKING ON HERE?
MY HOMEWORK. WE HAVE TO WRITE A STORY ABOUT THE RENAISSANCE TIME PERIOD. I WANTED TO DRAW SOME PICTURES WITH MY STORY AND MAKE IT A COMIC!
LOOKS LIKE YOU MIGHT NEED A NEW PENCIL. YOU'VE USED THIS ONE DOWN TO THE ERASER. I'VE GOT SOME SPARES IN MY BAG FROM THE DIG. RUN IN THE LIVING ROOM AND GRAB ONE.
OK! THANKS, DAD! I CAN'T WAIT TO FINISH THIS STORY. I'M ALMOST TO THE MONSTER PART.
OK, BUT AFTER YOU DRAW THE MONSTER, IT'S BEDTIME. OR YOUR MOM WILL BE THE MONSTER!

Alex's dad is an archaeologist. He studies cultures and history through artifacts from the past.

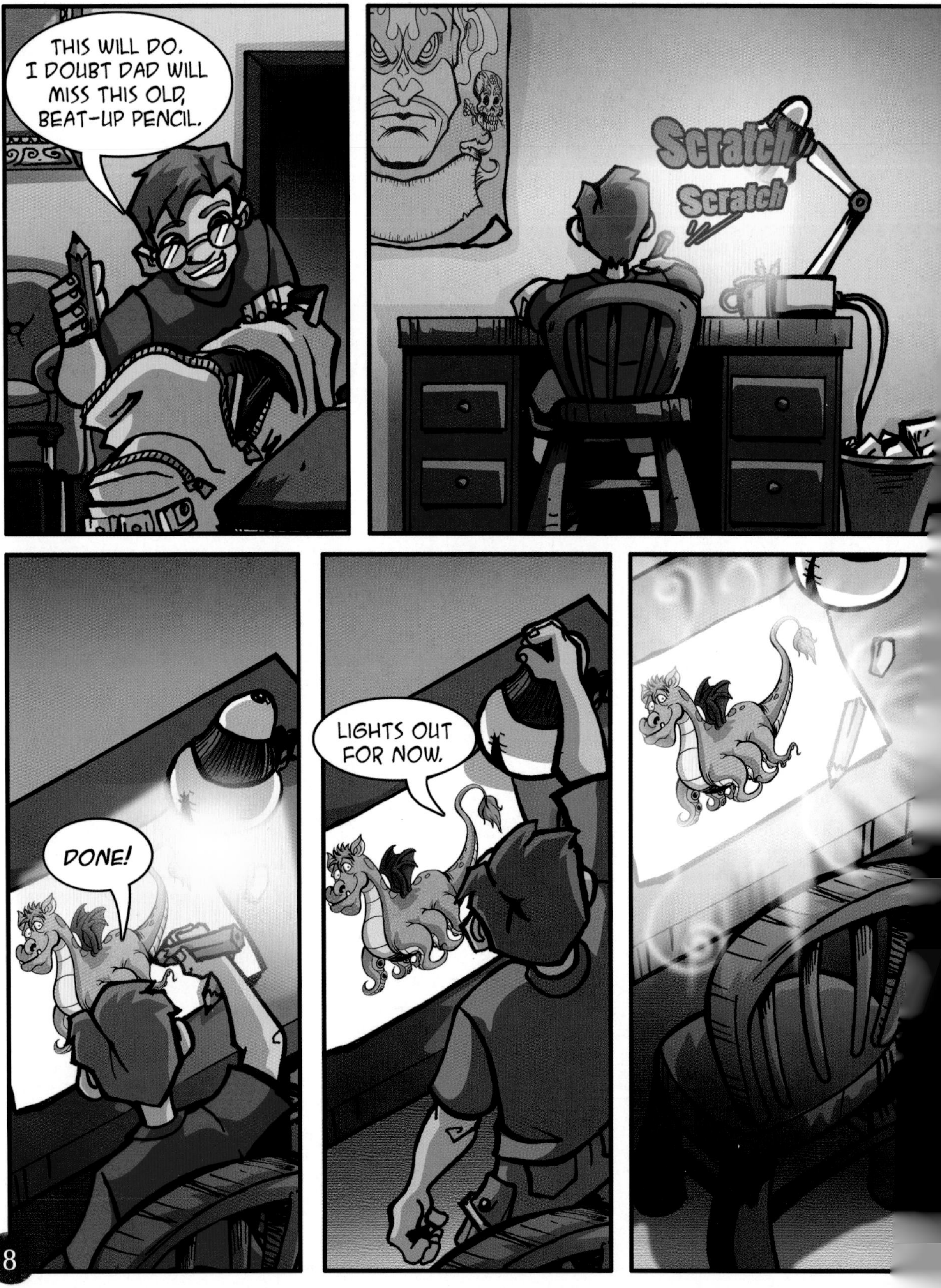
THIS WILL DO. I DOUBT DAD WILL MISS THIS OLD, BEAT-UP PENCIL.
Scratch, Scratch
DONE!
LIGHTS OUT FOR NOW.

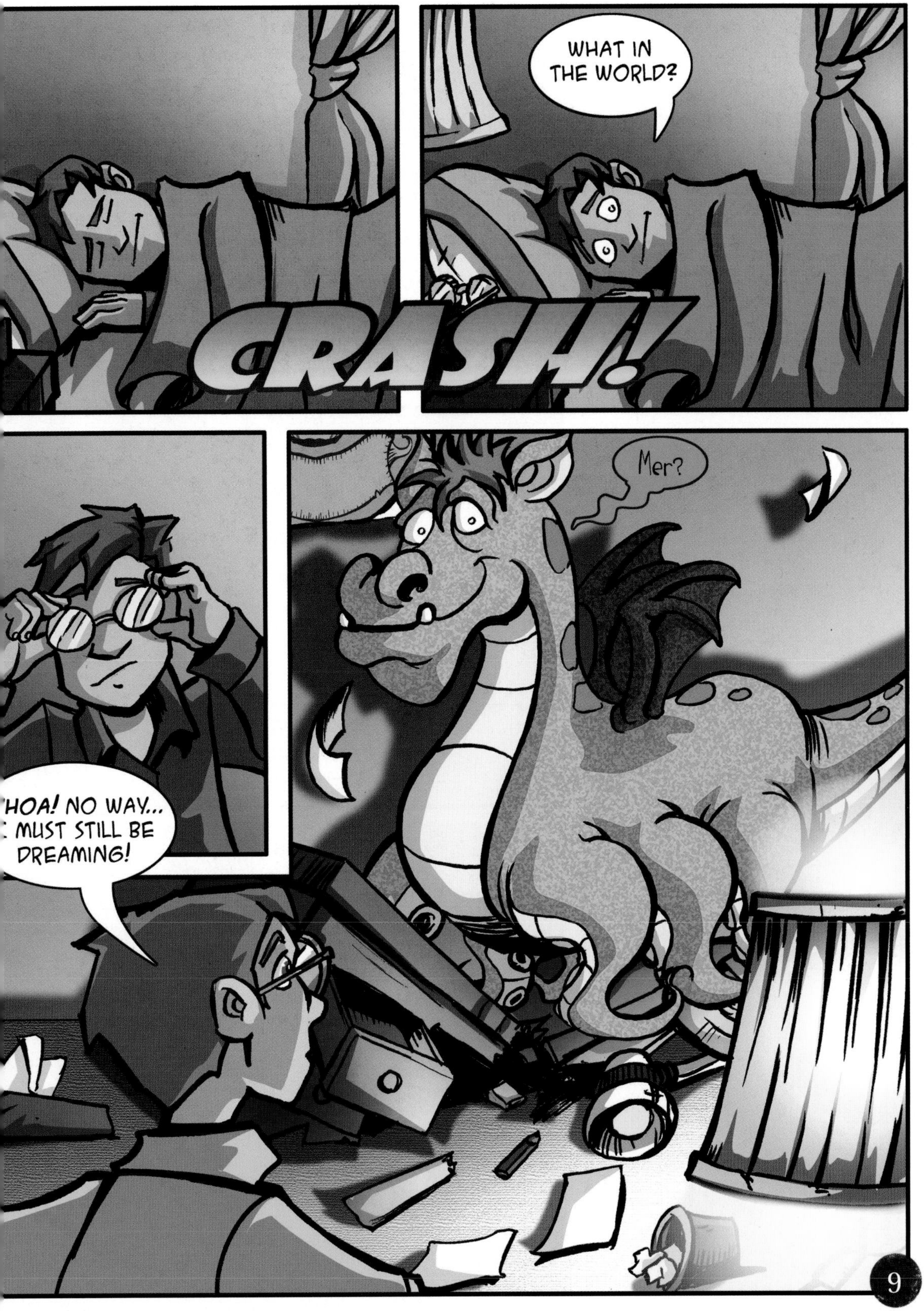
CRASH!
WHAT IN THE WORLD?
Mer?
HOA! NO WAY... MUST STILL BE DREAMING!

EVERYTHING OKAY IN THERE?

YEAH, MOM. UH...SORRY. I JUST DROPPED SOMETHING.

IT'S EARLY. ARE YOU SURE EVERYTHING IS OKAY?

UH-HUH. I JUST...WANTED TO GET AN EARLY START FOR THE RENAISSANCE FAIR TODAY IS ALL. HA HA.

OK, WELL TRY AND KEEP IT DOWN.

YOU WERE ON MY PAPER, AND NOW YOU'RE IN MY ROOM.

NOW, WHERE DID YOU COME FROM?

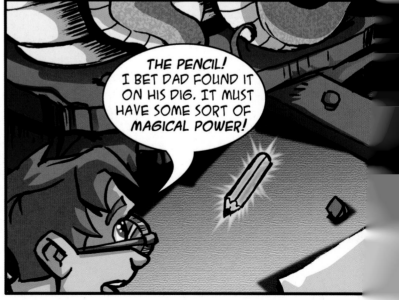

THE PENCIL! I BET DAD FOUND IT ON HIS DIG. IT MUST HAVE SOME SORT OF MAGICAL POWER!

10

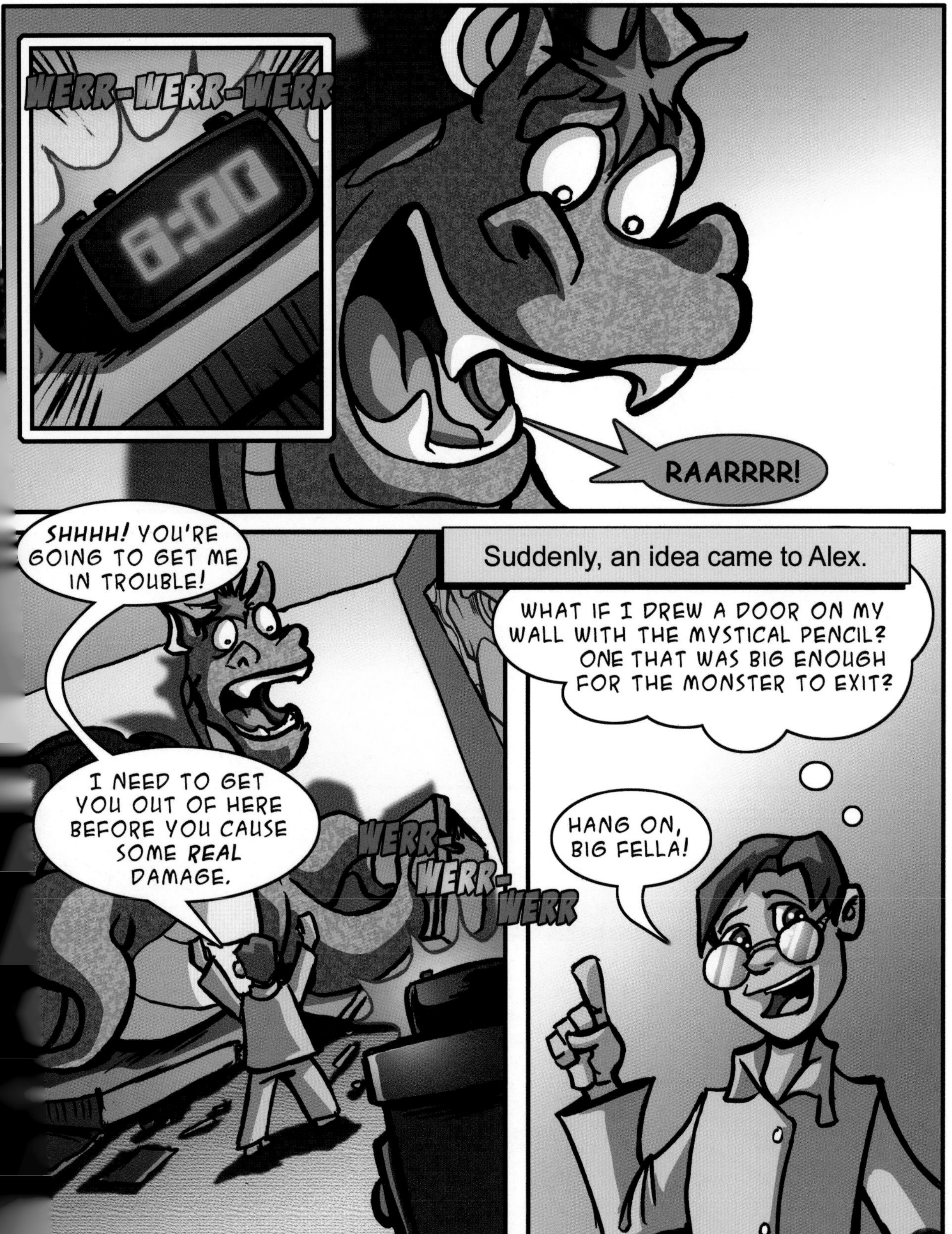
WERR-WERR-WERR
6:00
RAARRRR!
SHHHH! YOU'RE GOING TO GET ME IN TROUBLE!
I NEED TO GET YOU OUT OF HERE BEFORE YOU CAUSE SOME REAL DAMAGE.
WERR-WERR-WERR
Suddenly, an idea came to Alex.
WHAT IF I DREW A DOOR ON MY WALL WITH THE MYSTICAL PENCIL? ONE THAT WAS BIG ENOUGH FOR THE MONSTER TO EXIT?
HANG ON, BIG FELLA!

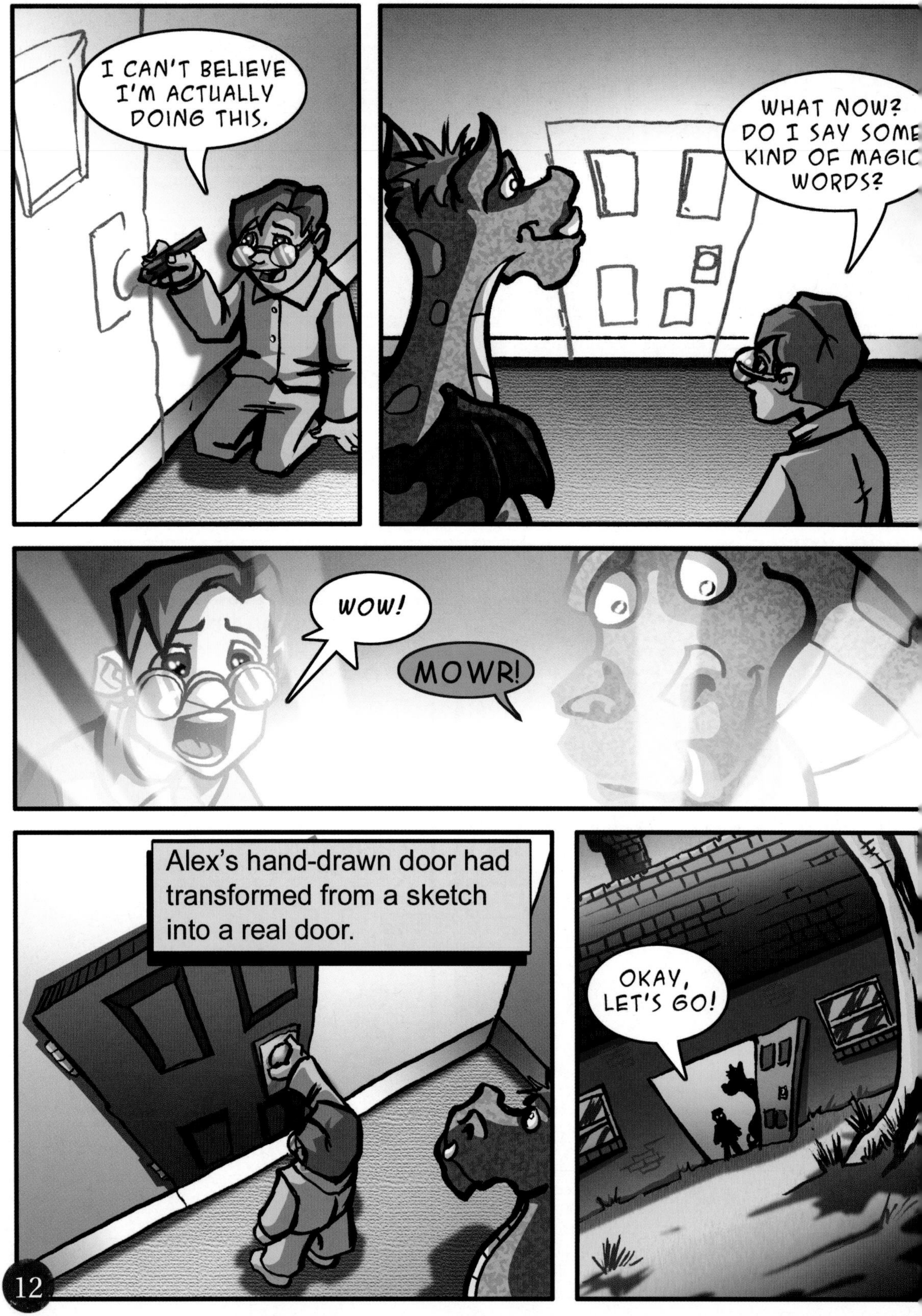
I CAN'T BELIEVE I'M ACTUALLY DOING THIS.
WHAT NOW? DO I SAY SOME KIND OF MAGIC WORDS?
WOW!
MOWR!
Alex's hand-drawn door had transformed from a sketch into a real door.
OKAY, LET'S GO!

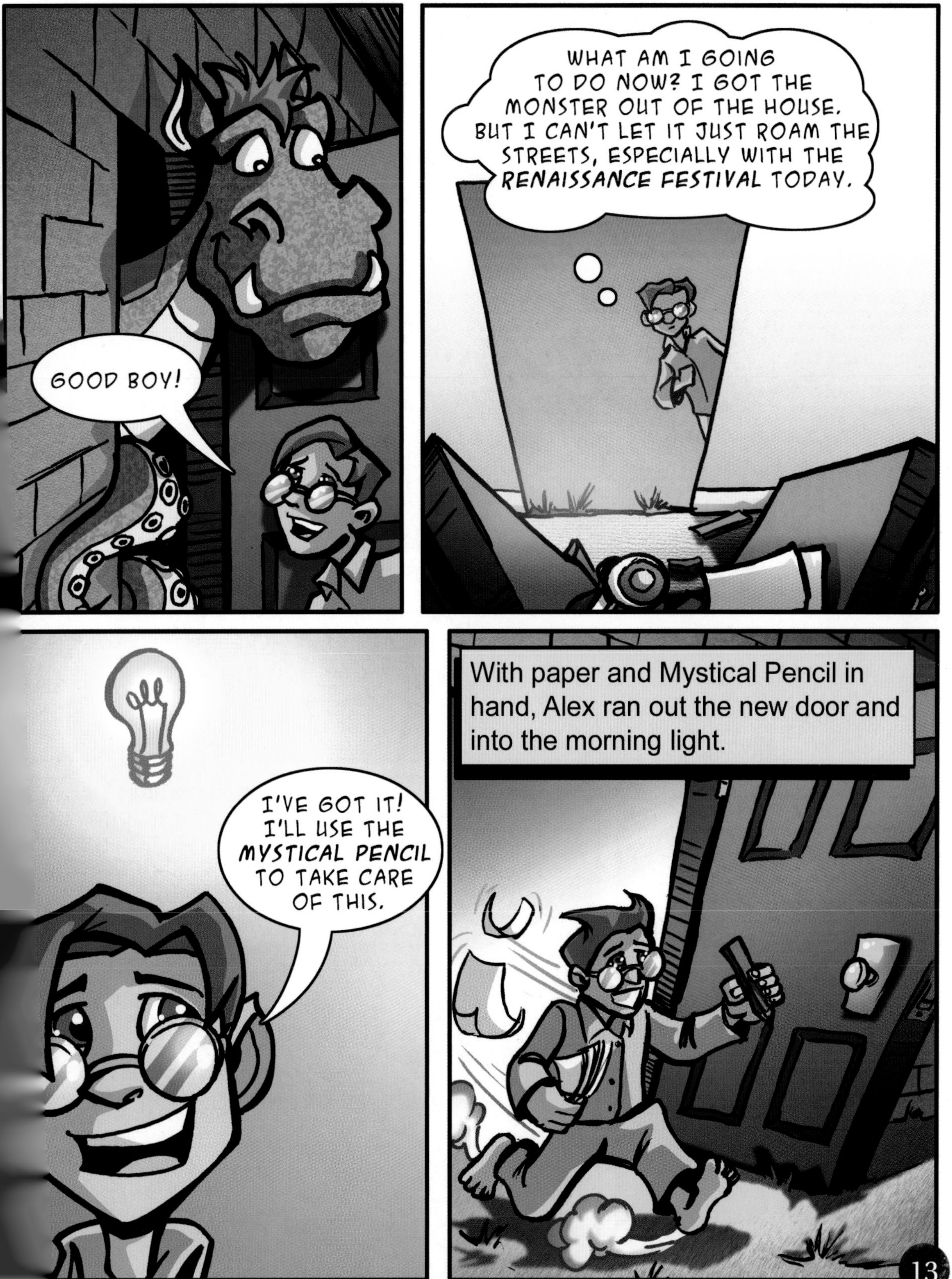
GOOD BOY!
WHAT AM I GOING TO DO NOW? I GOT THE MONSTER OUT OF THE HOUSE. BUT I CAN'T LET IT JUST ROAM THE STREETS, ESPECIALLY WITH THE RENAISSANCE FESTIVAL TODAY.
I'VE GOT IT! I'LL USE THE MYSTICAL PENCIL TO TAKE CARE OF THIS.
With paper and Mystical Pencil in hand, Alex ran out the new door and into the morning light.

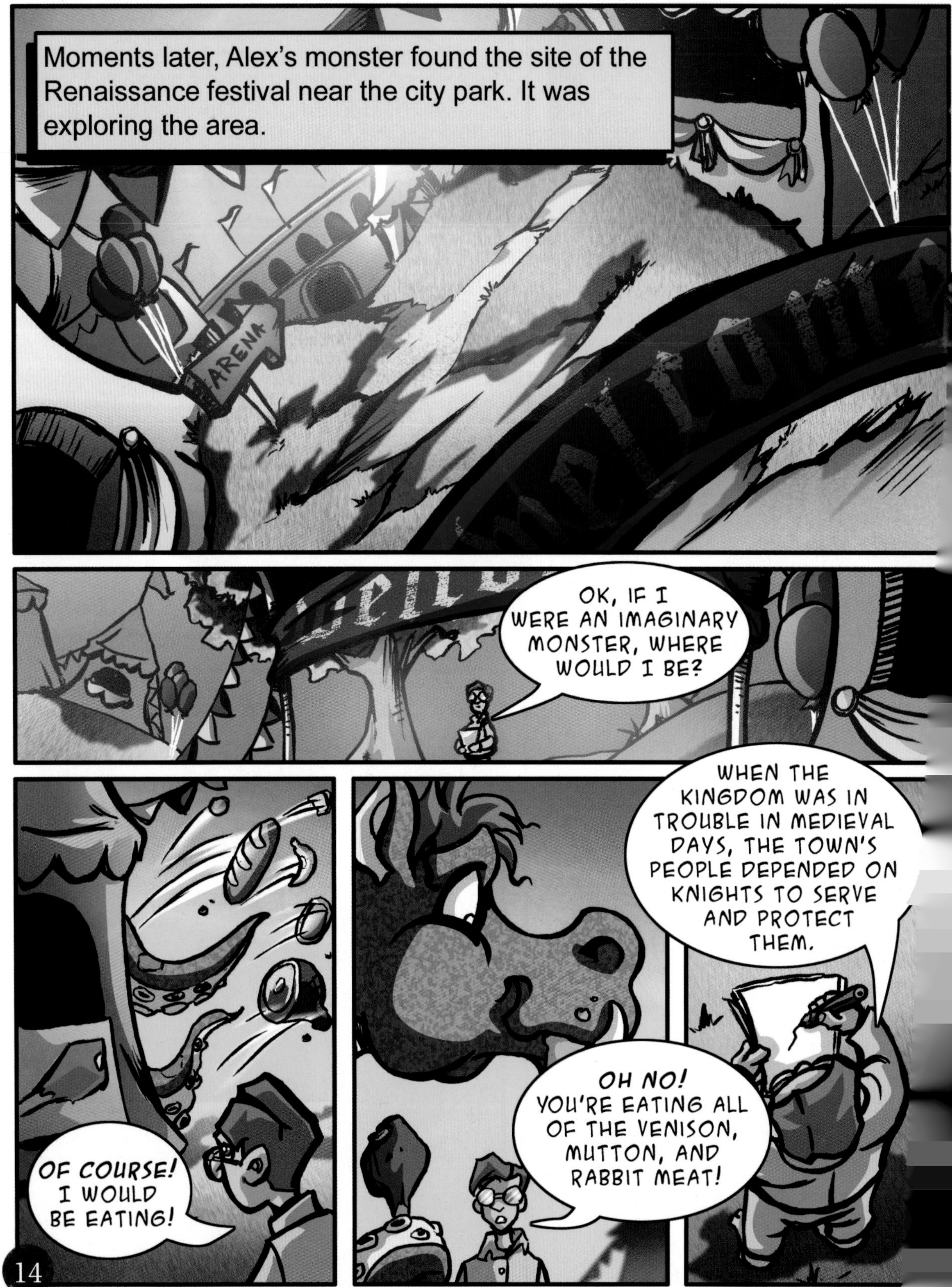
Moments later, Alex's monster found the site of the Renaissance festival near the city park. It was exploring the area.
ARENA
OK, IF I WERE AN IMAGINARY MONSTER, WHERE WOULD I BE?
OF COURSE! I WOULD BE EATING!
WHEN THE KINGDOM WAS IN TROUBLE IN MEDIEVAL DAYS, THE TOWN'S PEOPLE DEPENDED ON KNIGHTS TO SERVE AND PROTECT THEM.
OH NO! YOU'RE EATING ALL OF THE VENISON, MUTTON, AND RABBIT MEAT!

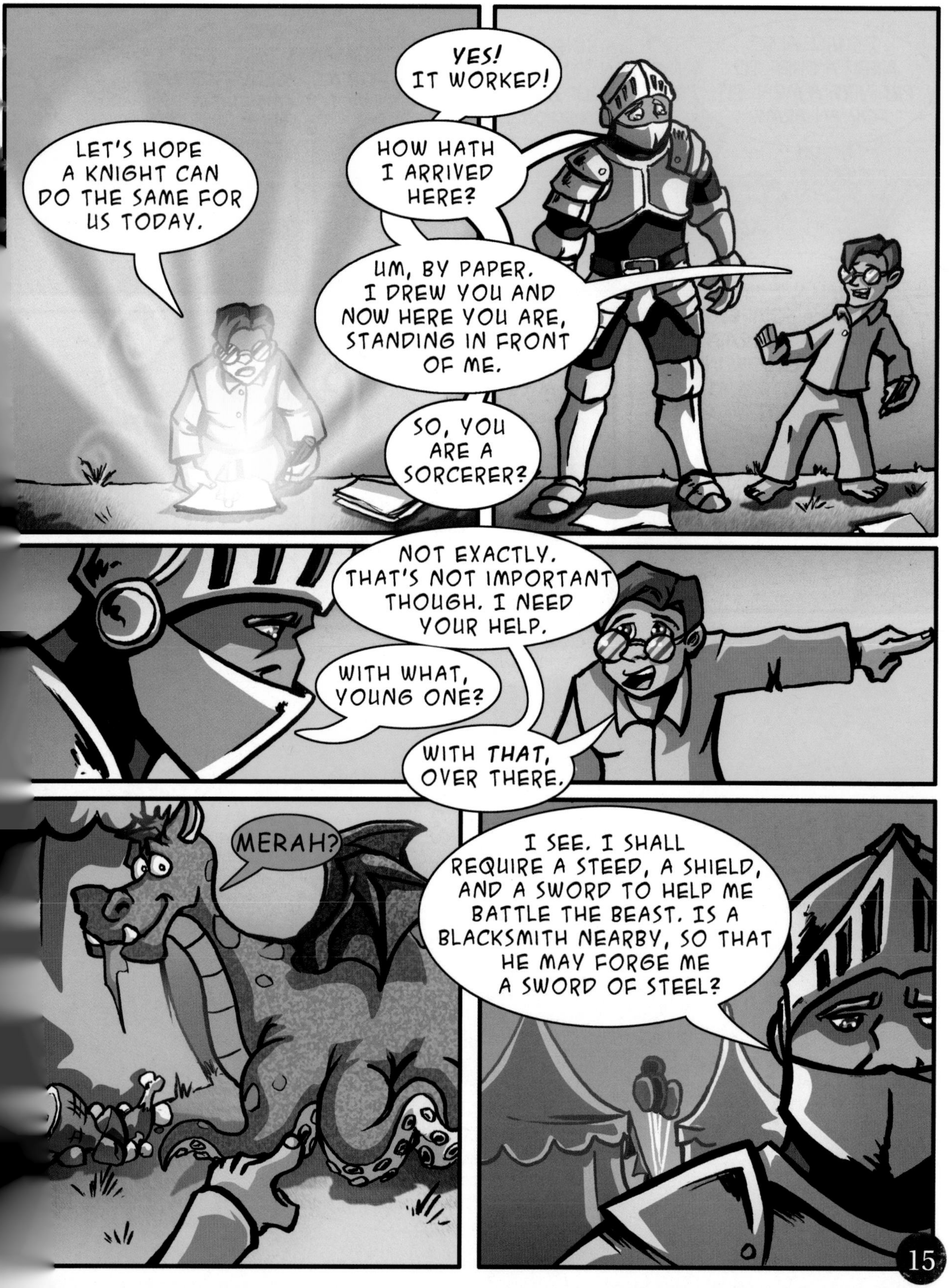
LET'S HOPE A KNIGHT CAN DO THE SAME FOR US TODAY.
YES! IT WORKED!
HOW HATH I ARRIVED HERE?
UM, BY PAPER. I DREW YOU AND NOW HERE YOU ARE, STANDING IN FRONT OF ME.
SO, YOU ARE A SORCERER?
NOT EXACTLY. THAT'S NOT IMPORTANT THOUGH. I NEED YOUR HELP.
WITH WHAT, YOUNG ONE?
WITH THAT, OVER THERE.
MERAH?
I SEE. I SHALL REQUIRE A STEED, A SHIELD, AND A SWORD TO HELP ME BATTLE THE BEAST. IS A BLACKSMITH NEARBY, SO THAT HE MAY FORGE ME A SWORD OF STEEL?

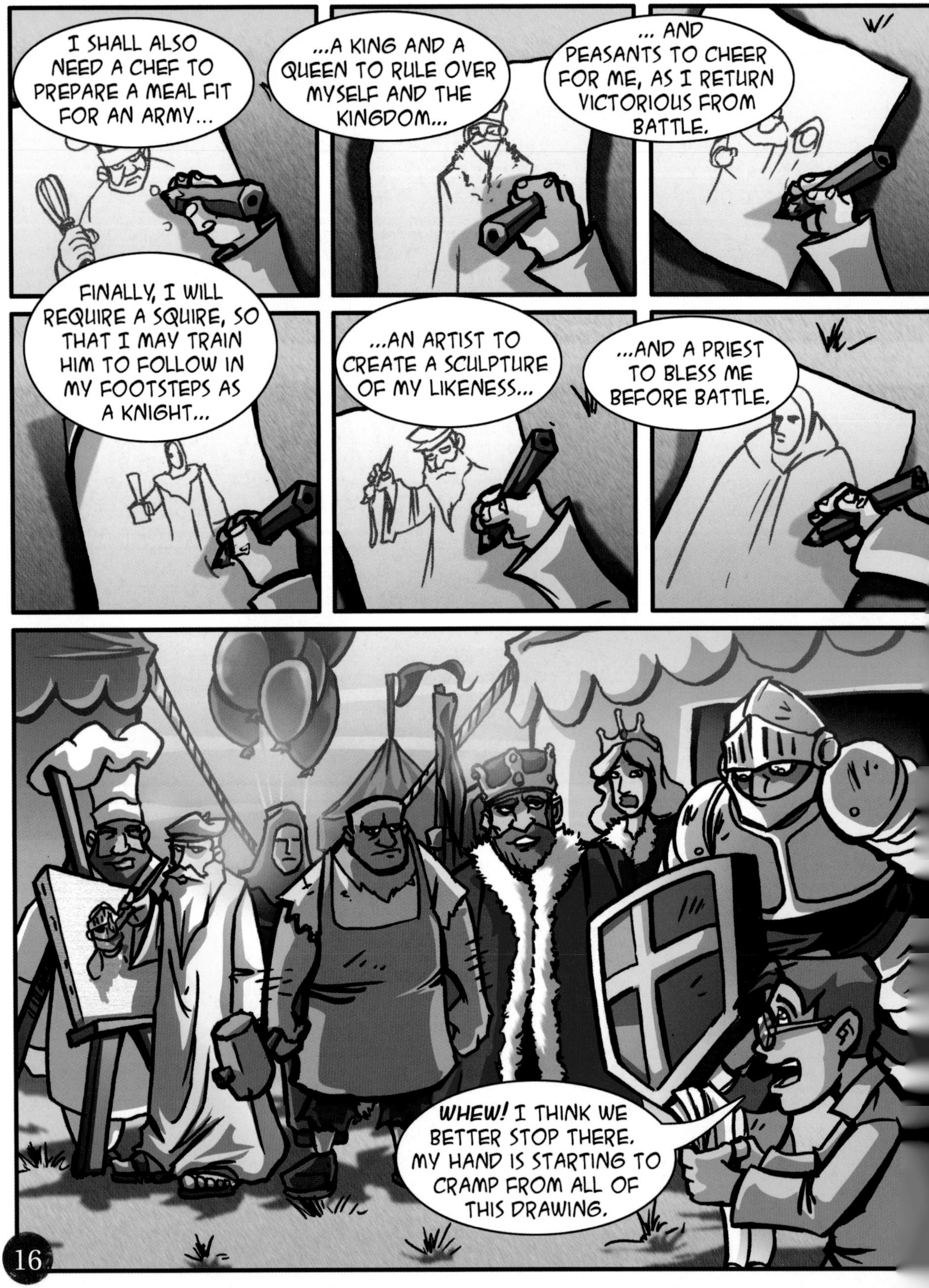
I SHALL ALSO NEED A CHEF TO PREPARE A MEAL FIT FOR AN ARMY...
...A KING AND A QUEEN TO RULE OVER MYSELF AND THE KINGDOM...
... AND PEASANTS TO CHEER FOR ME, AS I RETURN VICTORIOUS FROM BATTLE.
FINALLY, I WILL REQUIRE A SQUIRE, SO THAT I MAY TRAIN HIM TO FOLLOW IN MY FOOTSTEPS AS A KNIGHT...
...AN ARTIST TO CREATE A SCULPTURE OF MY LIKENESS...
...AND A PRIEST TO BLESS ME BEFORE BATTLE.
WHEW! I THINK WE BETTER STOP THERE. MY HAND IS STARTING TO CRAMP FROM ALL OF THIS DRAWING.

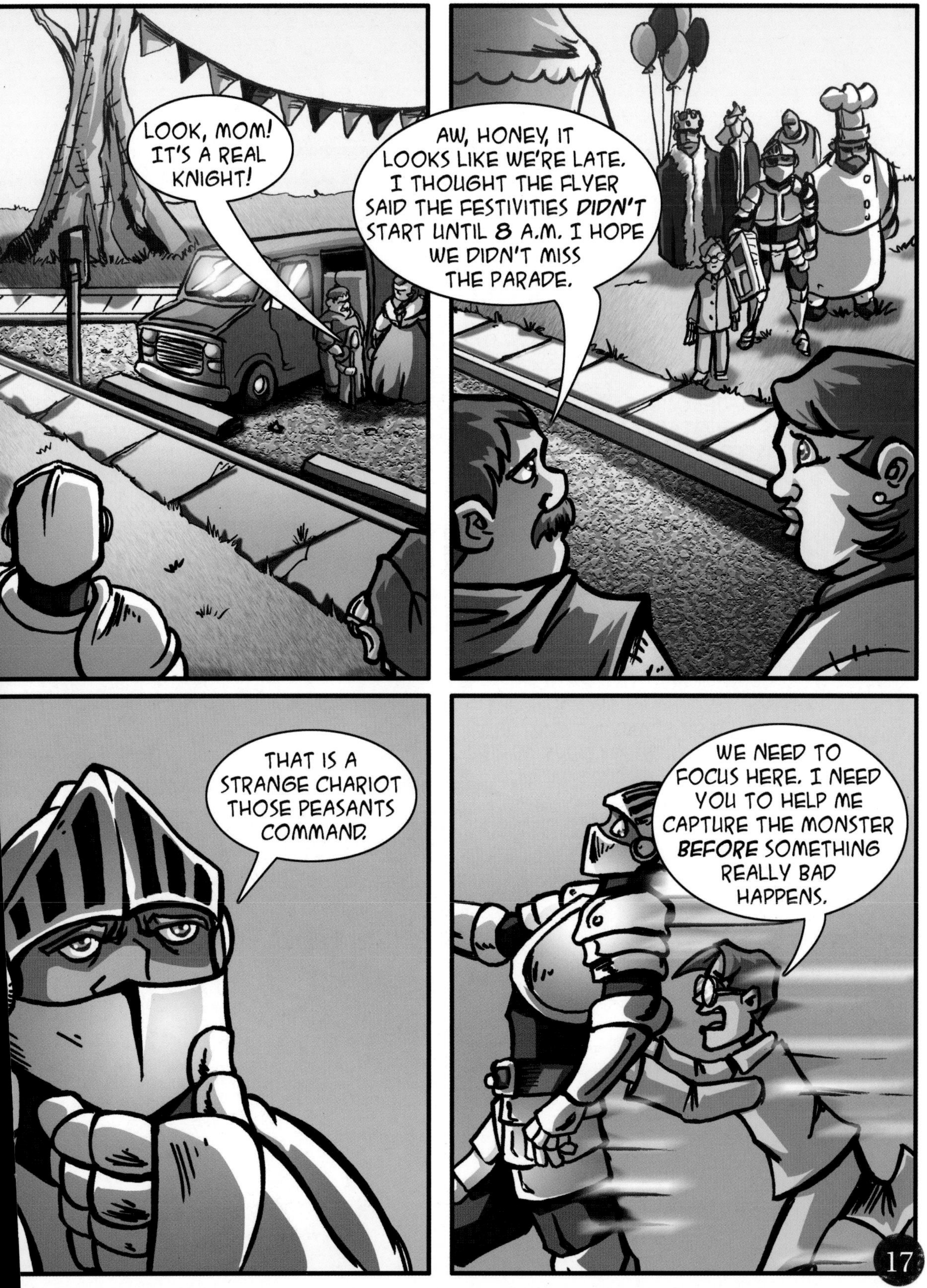
LOOK, MOM! IT'S A REAL KNIGHT!
AW, HONEY, IT LOOKS LIKE WE'RE LATE. I THOUGHT THE FLYER SAID THE FESTIVITIES *DIDN'T* START UNTIL 8 A.M. I HOPE WE DIDN'T MISS THE PARADE.
THAT IS A STRANGE CHARIOT THOSE PEASANTS COMMAND.
WE NEED TO FOCUS HERE. I NEED YOU TO HELP ME CAPTURE THE MONSTER *BEFORE* SOMETHING REALLY BAD HAPPENS.

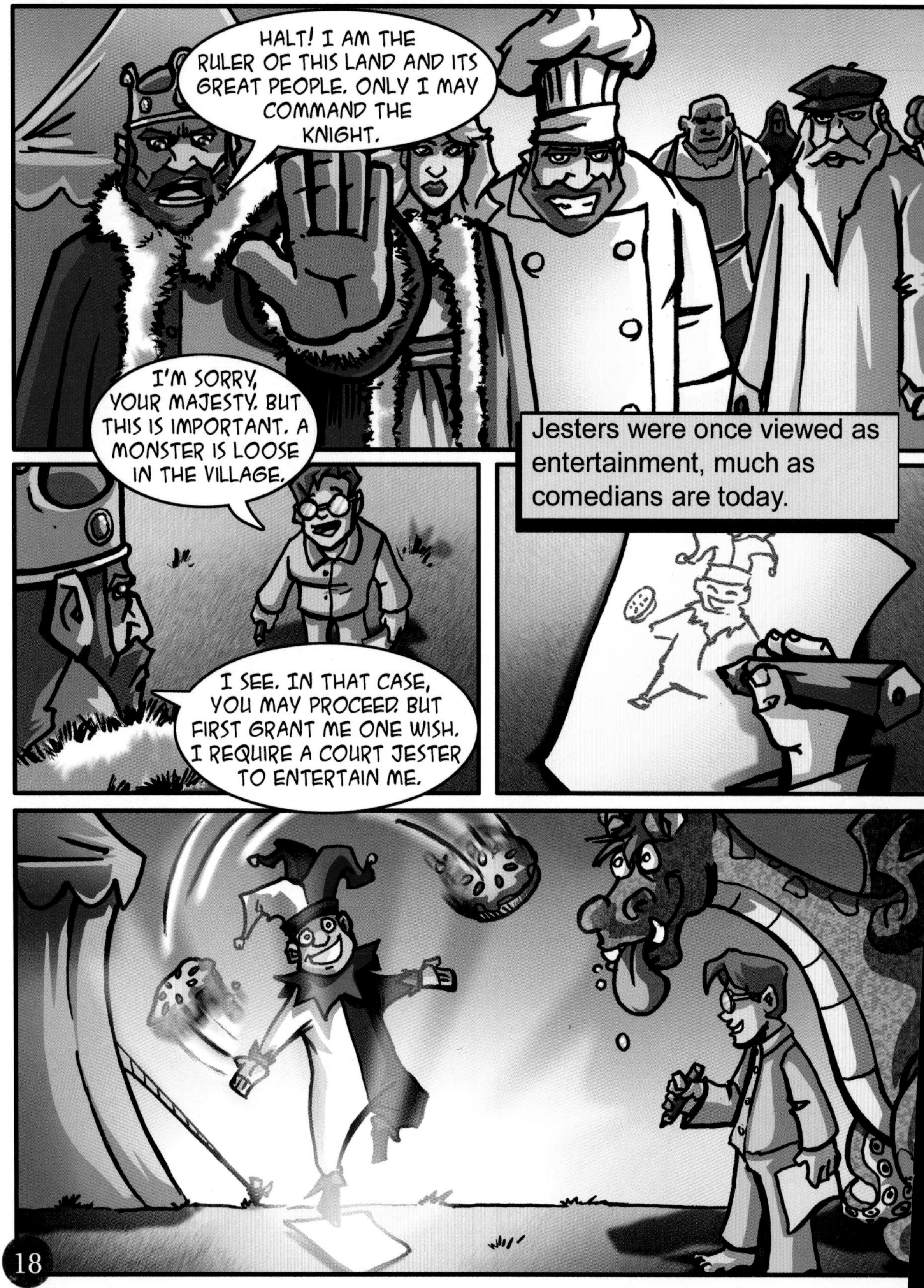
HALT! I AM THE RULER OF THIS LAND AND ITS GREAT PEOPLE. ONLY I MAY COMMAND THE KNIGHT.
I'M SORRY, YOUR MAJESTY. BUT THIS IS IMPORTANT. A MONSTER IS LOOSE IN THE VILLAGE.
Jesters were once viewed as entertainment, much as comedians are today.
I SEE. IN THAT CASE, YOU MAY PROCEED. BUT FIRST GRANT ME ONE WISH. I REQUIRE A COURT JESTER TO ENTERTAIN ME.

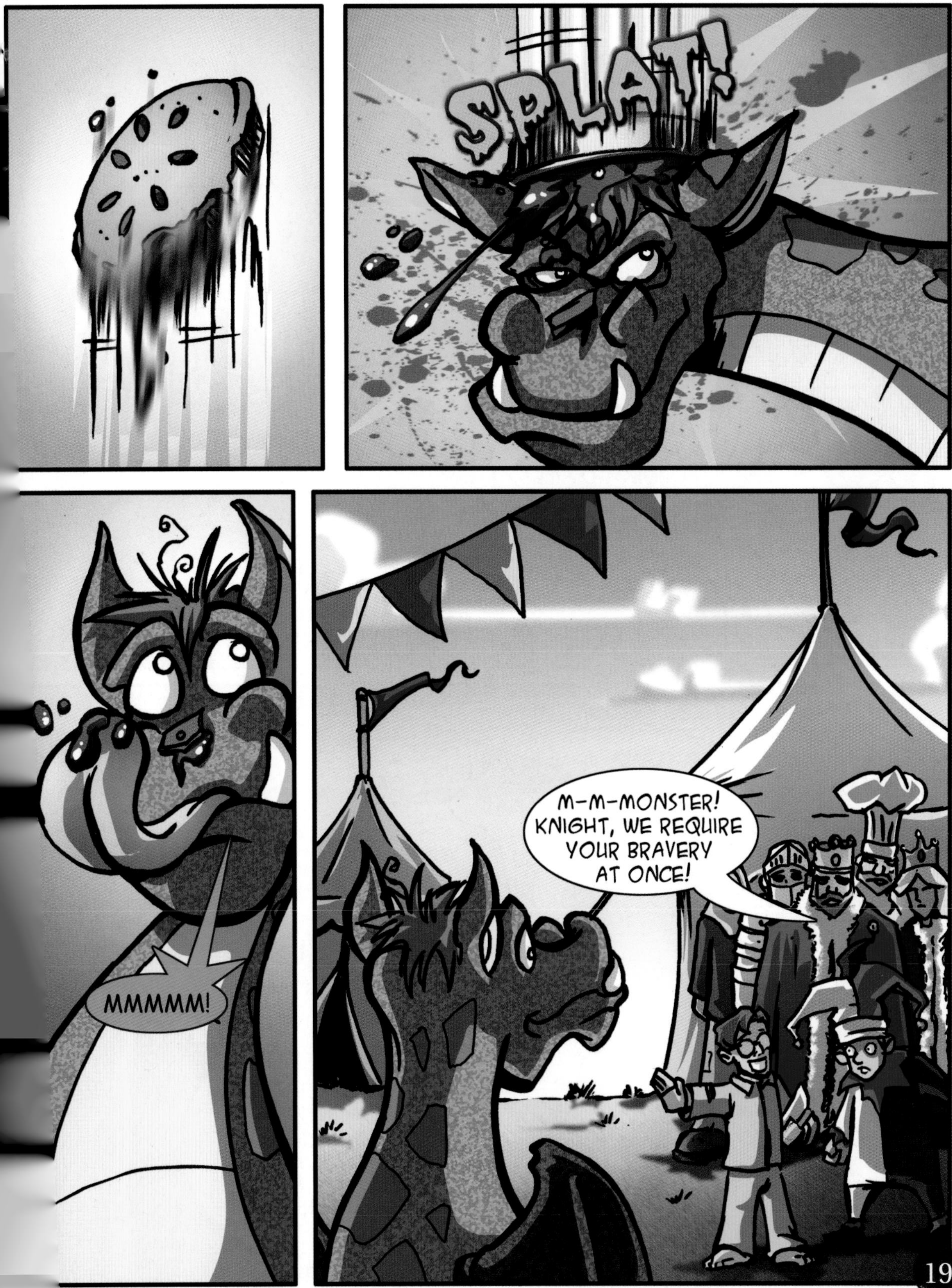
SPLAT!
MMMMM!
M-M-MONSTER! KNIGHT, WE REQUIRE YOUR BRAVERY AT ONCE!

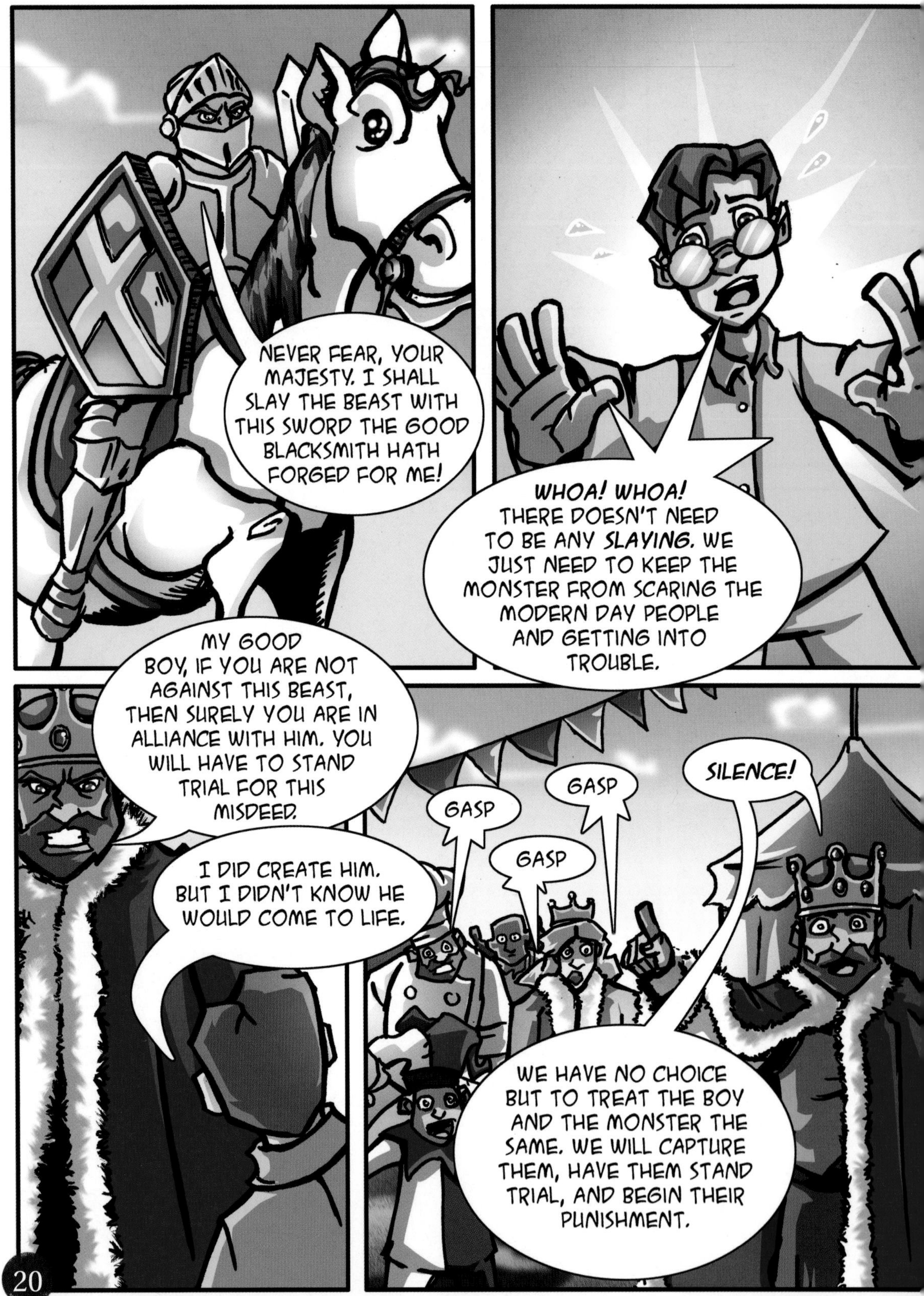
NEVER FEAR, YOUR MAJESTY. I SHALL SLAY THE BEAST WITH THIS SWORD THE GOOD BLACKSMITH HATH FORGED FOR ME!
WHOA! WHOA! THERE DOESN'T NEED TO BE ANY SLAYING. WE JUST NEED TO KEEP THE MONSTER FROM SCARING THE MODERN DAY PEOPLE AND GETTING INTO TROUBLE.
MY GOOD BOY, IF YOU ARE NOT AGAINST THIS BEAST, THEN SURELY YOU ARE IN ALLIANCE WITH HIM. YOU WILL HAVE TO STAND TRIAL FOR THIS MISDEED.
I DID CREATE HIM. BUT I DIDN'T KNOW HE WOULD COME TO LIFE.
GASP
GASP
GASP
SILENCE!
WE HAVE NO CHOICE BUT TO TREAT THE BOY AND THE MONSTER THE SAME. WE WILL CAPTURE THEM, HAVE THEM STAND TRIAL, AND BEGIN THEIR PUNISHMENT.

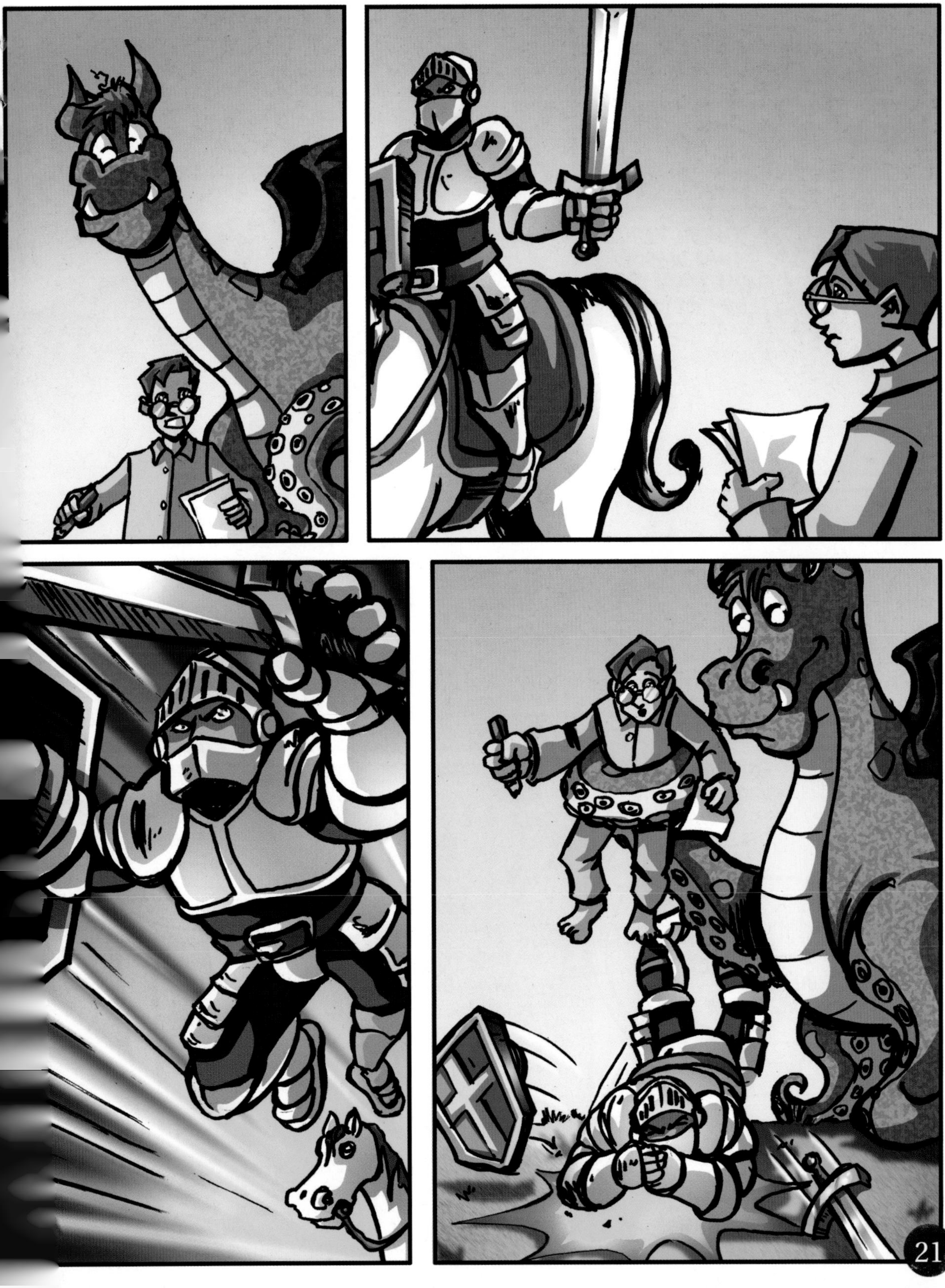

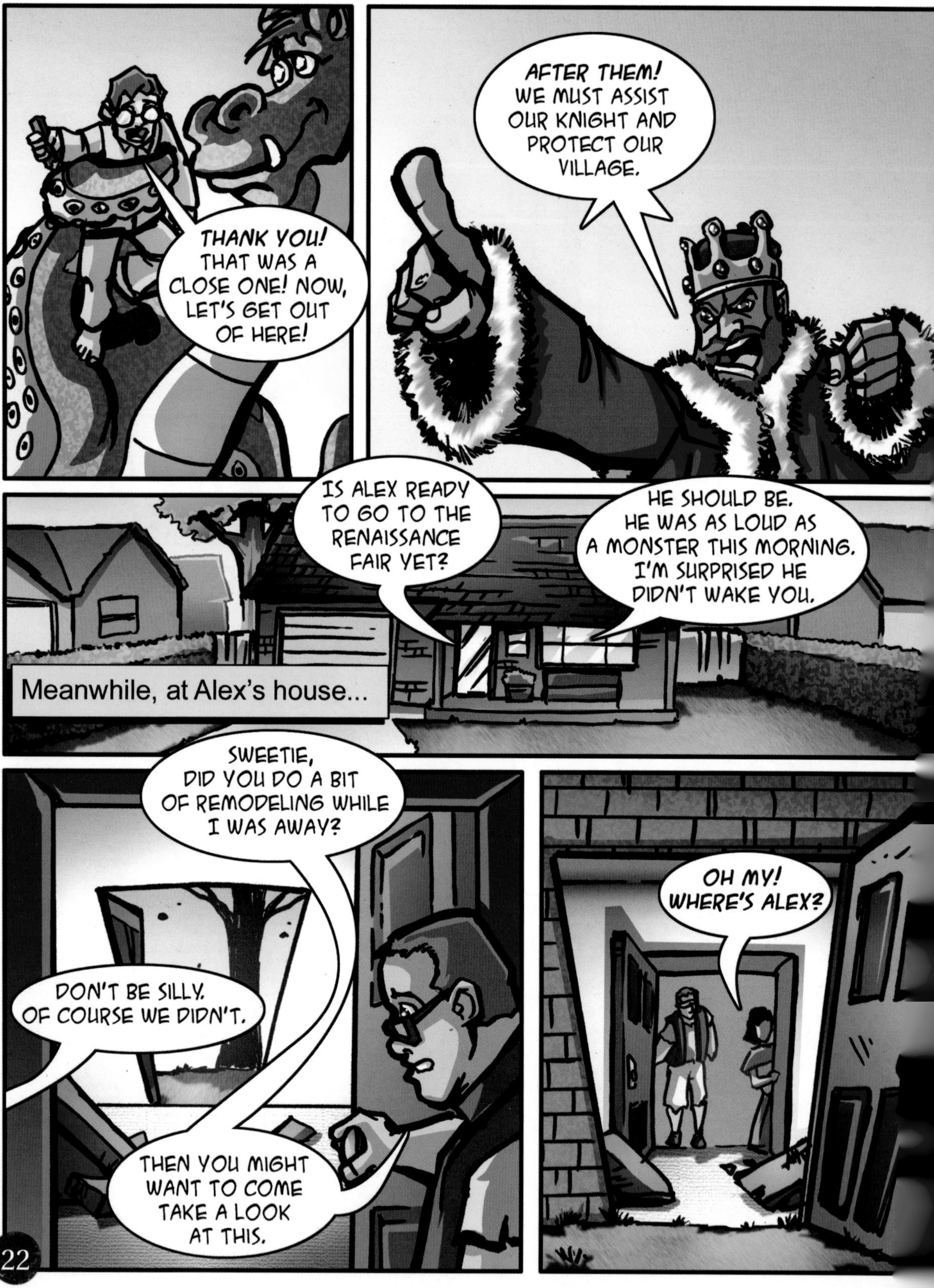
THANK YOU! THAT WAS A CLOSE ONE! NOW, LET'S GET OUT OF HERE!
AFTER THEM! WE MUST ASSIST OUR KNIGHT AND PROTECT OUR VILLAGE.
Meanwhile, at Alex's house...
IS ALEX READY TO GO TO THE RENAISSANCE FAIR YET?
HE SHOULD BE. HE WAS AS LOUD AS A MONSTER THIS MORNING. I'M SURPRISED HE DIDN'T WAKE YOU.
SWEETIE, DID YOU DO A BIT OF REMODELING WHILE I WAS AWAY?
DON'T BE SILLY. OF COURSE WE DIDN'T.
THEN YOU MIGHT WANT TO COME TAKE A LOOK AT THIS.
OH MY! WHERE'S ALEX?

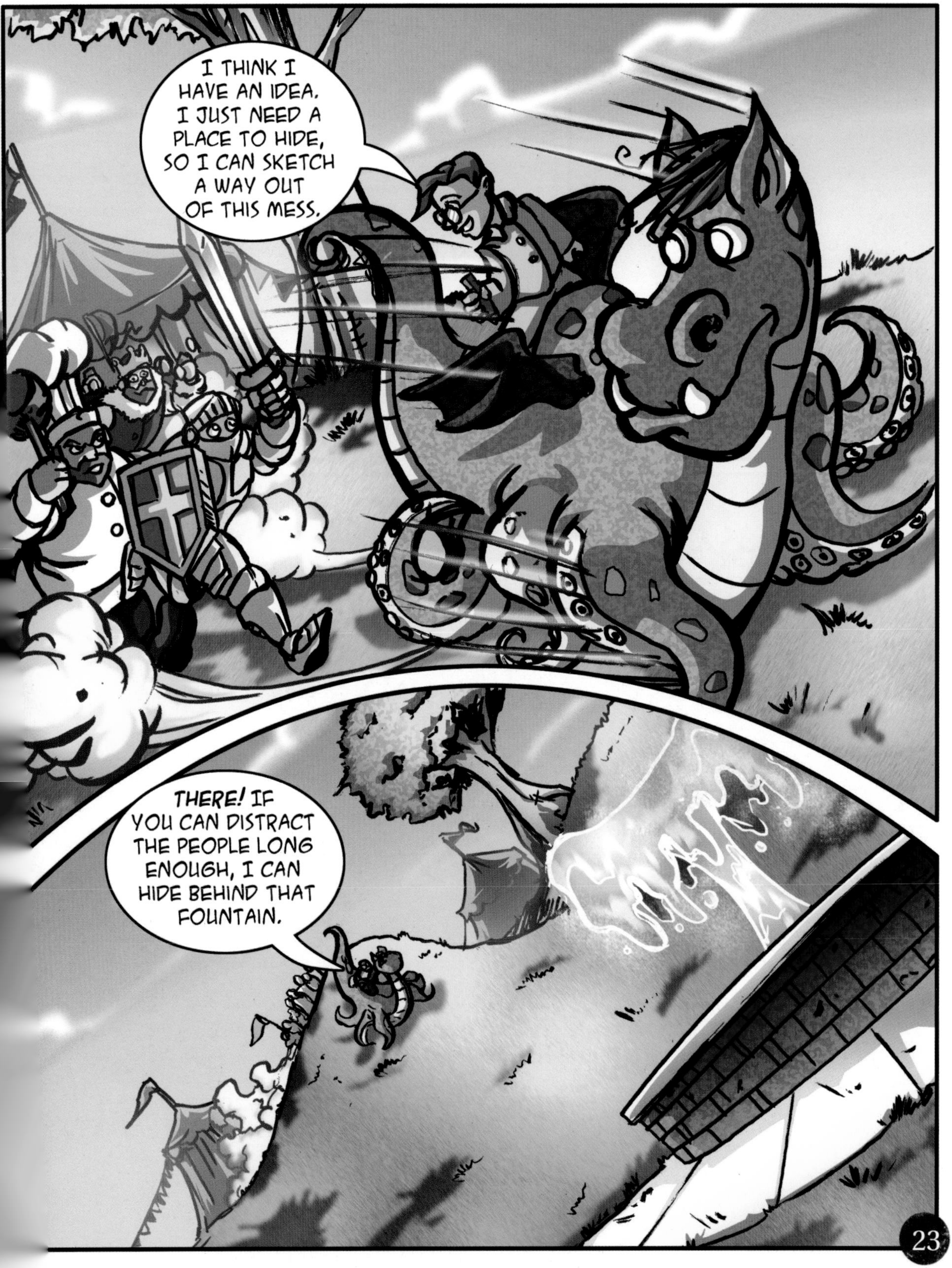
I THINK I HAVE AN IDEA. I JUST NEED A PLACE TO HIDE, SO I CAN SKETCH A WAY OUT OF THIS MESS.
THERE! IF YOU CAN DISTRACT THE PEOPLE LONG ENOUGH, I CAN HIDE BEHIND THAT FOUNTAIN.

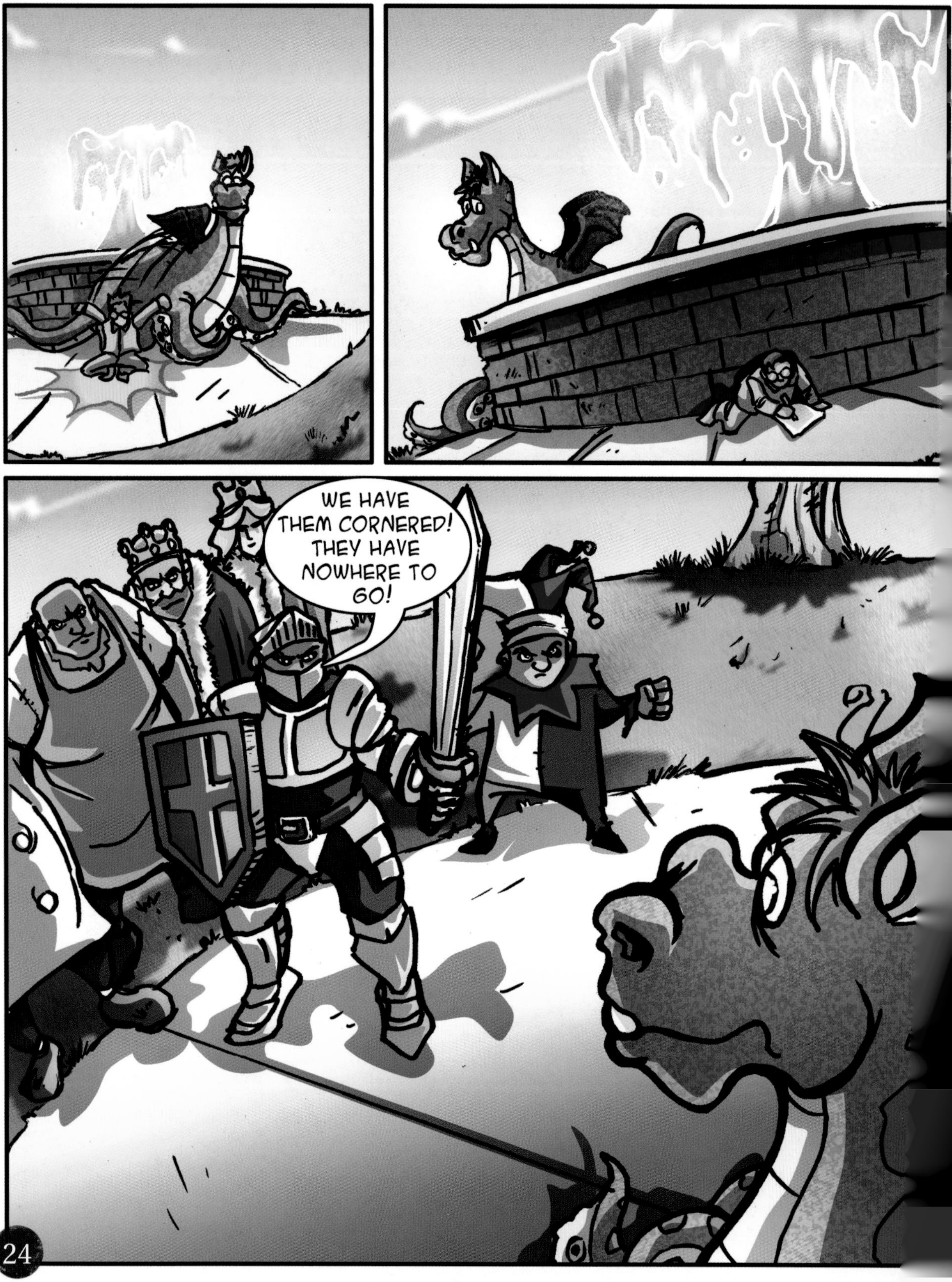
WE HAVE THEM CORNERED! THEY HAVE NOWHERE TO GO!

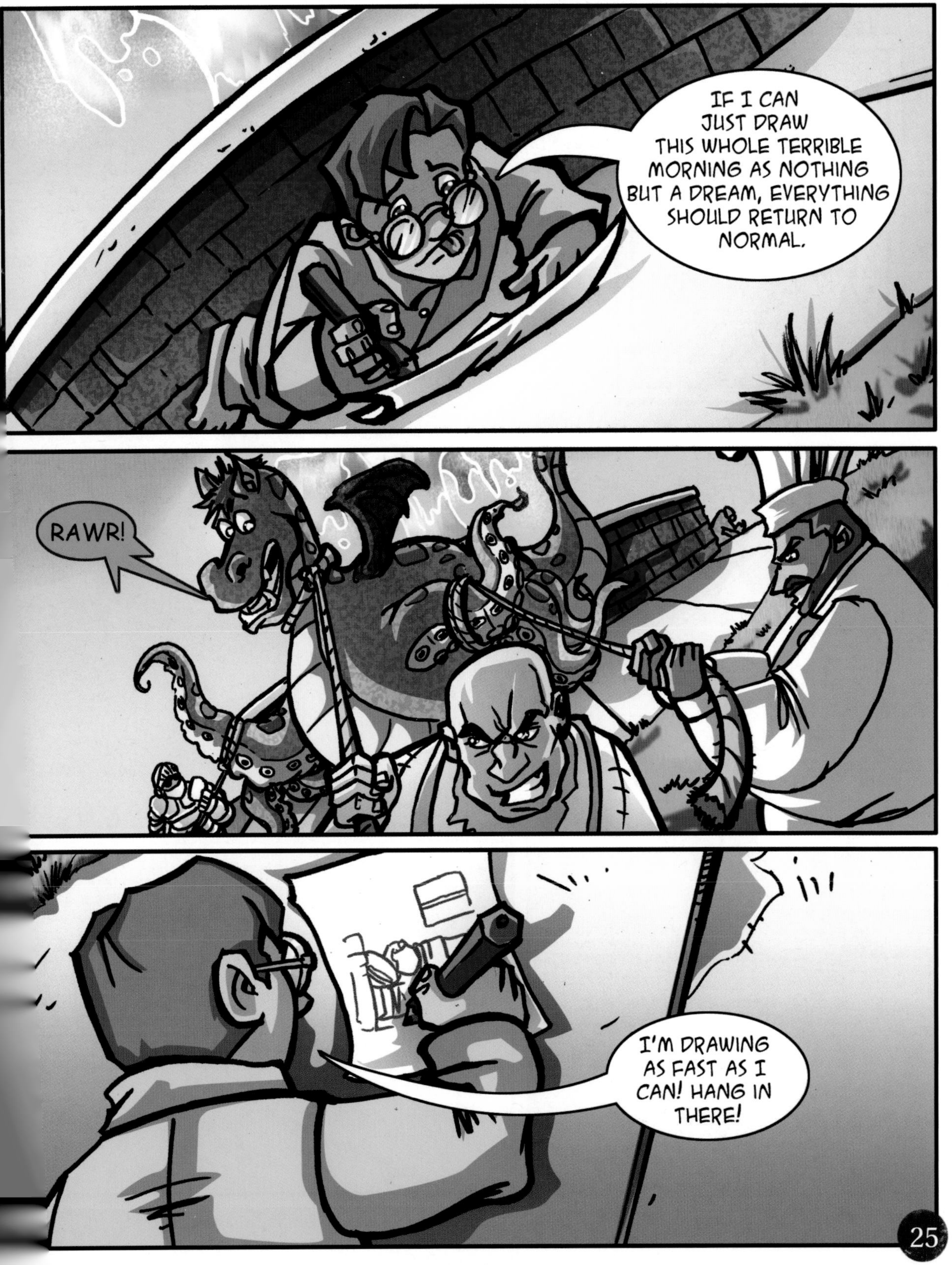
IF I CAN JUST DRAW THIS WHOLE TERRIBLE MORNING AS NOTHING BUT A DREAM, EVERYTHING SHOULD RETURN TO NORMAL.
RAWR!
I'M DRAWING AS FAST AS I CAN! HANG IN THERE!

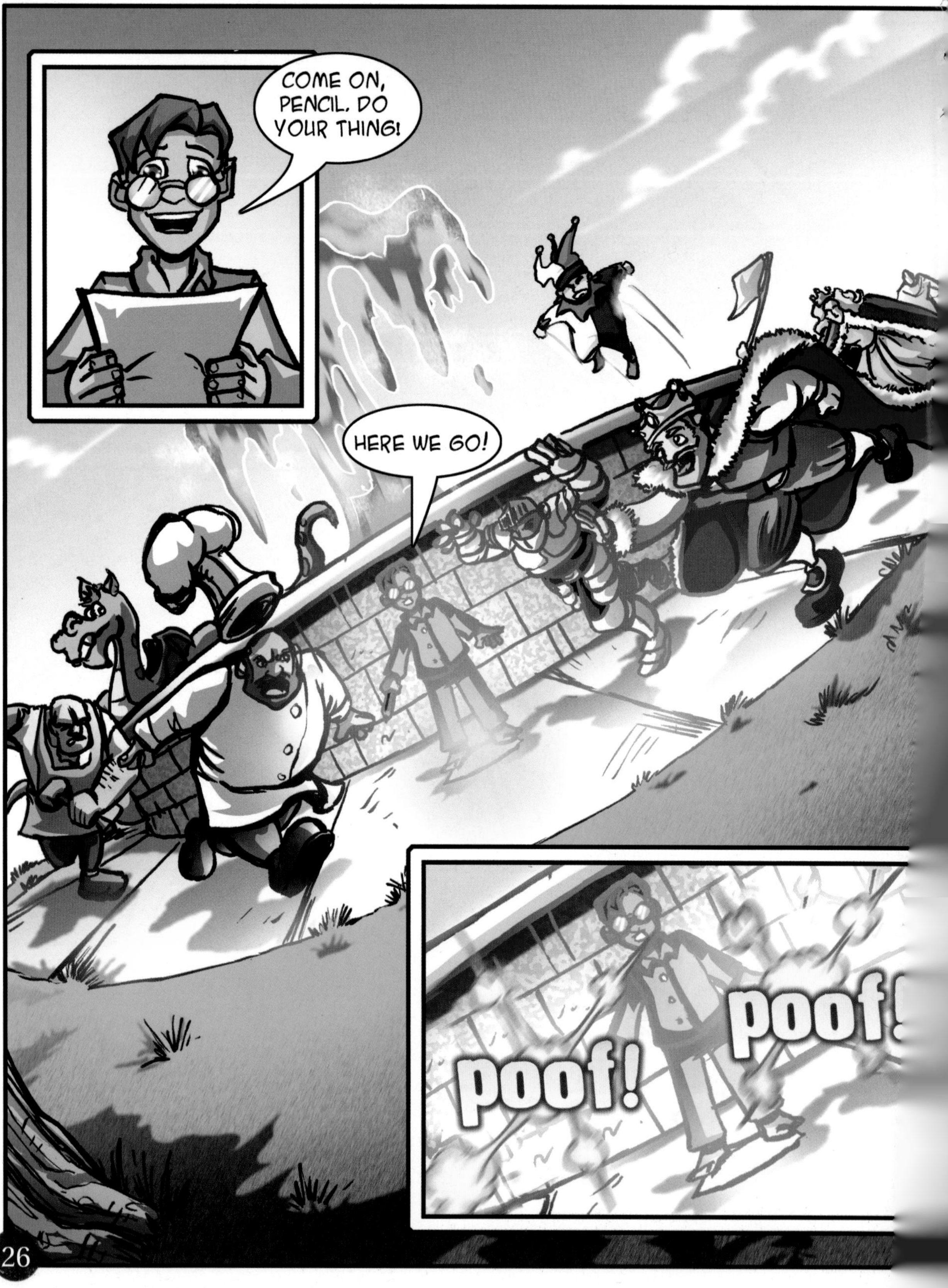
COME ON, PENCIL. DO YOUR THING!
HERE WE GO!
poof!
poof!

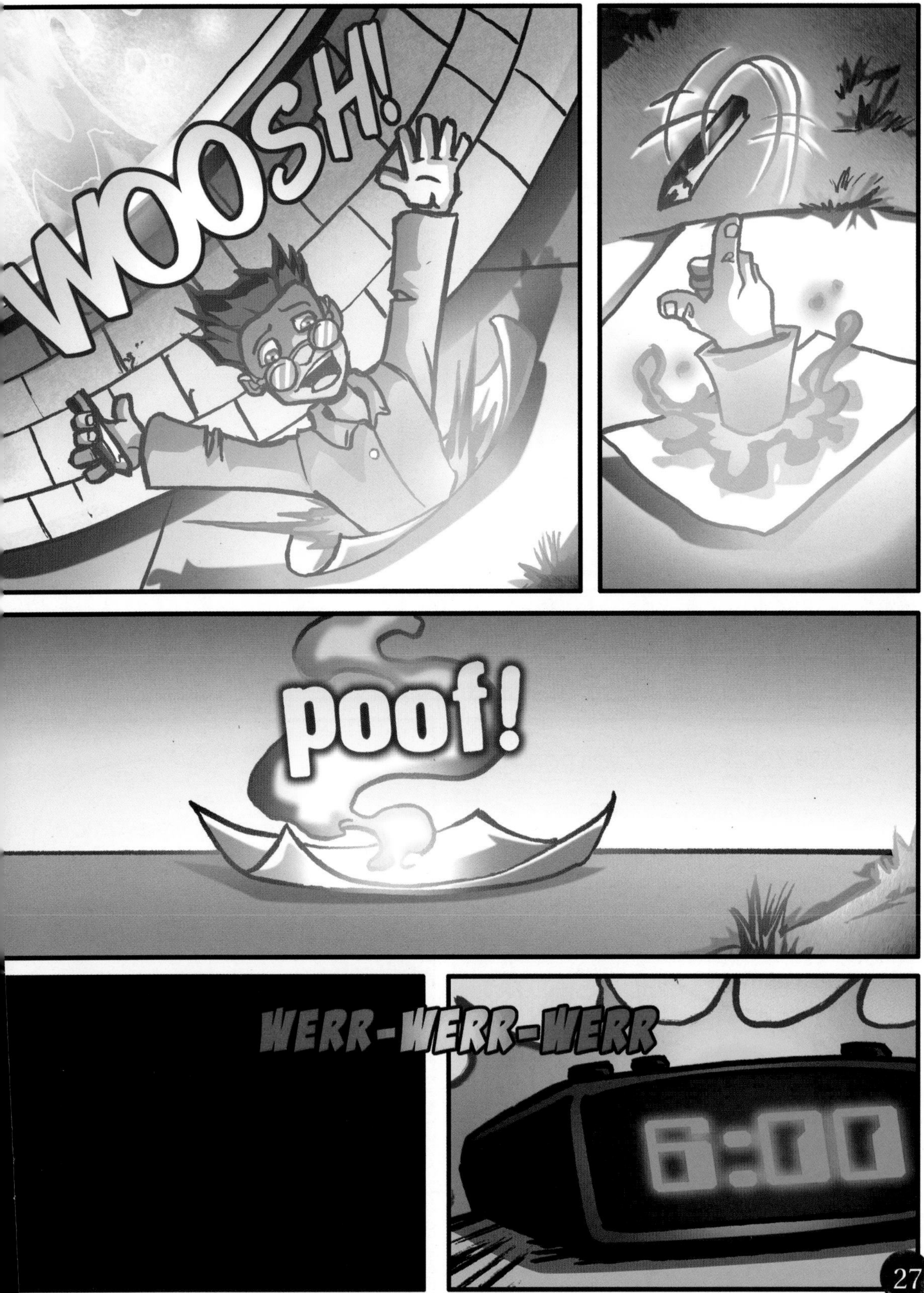
WOOSH!
poof!
WERR-WERR-WERR
6:00

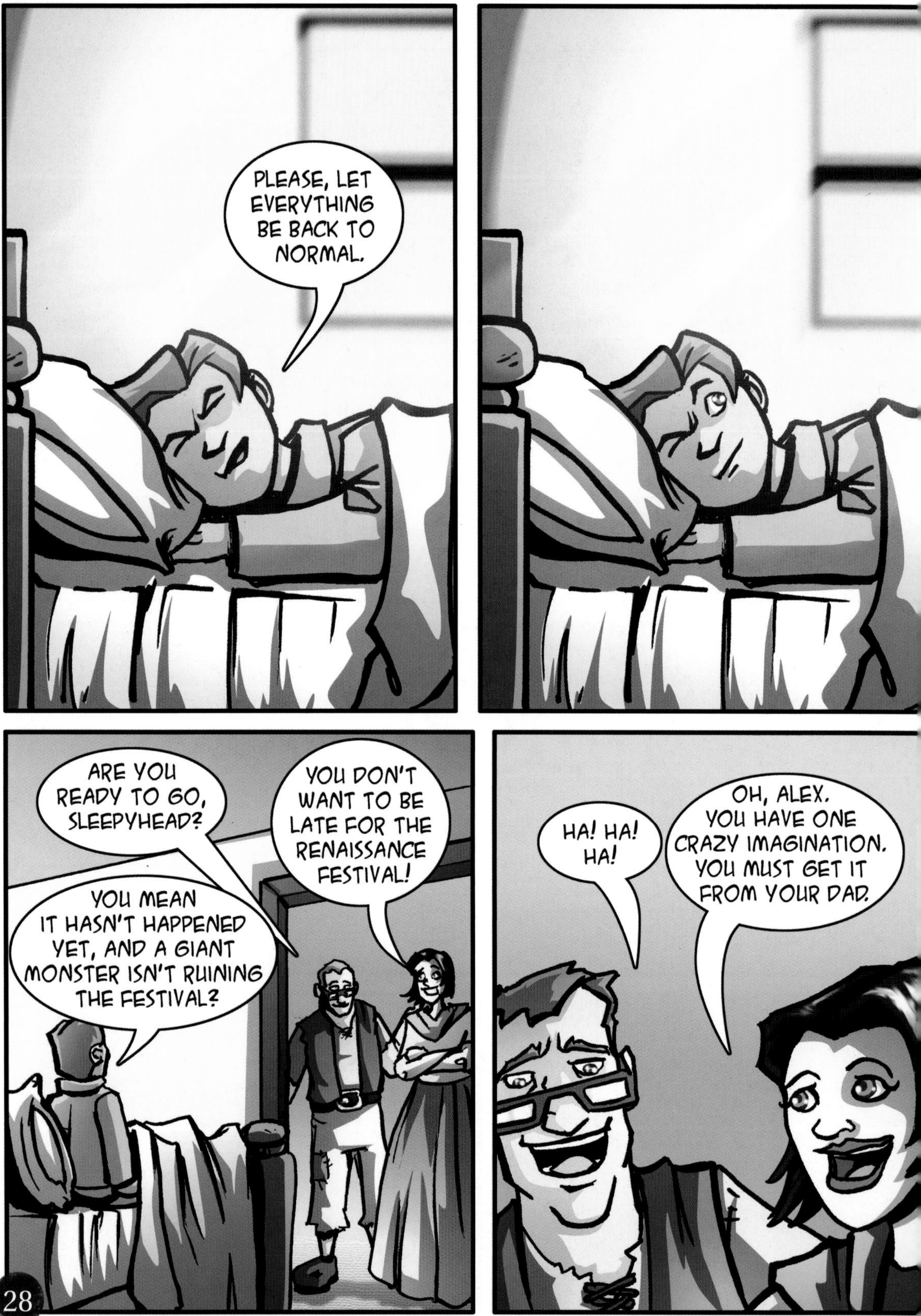
PLEASE, LET EVERYTHING BE BACK TO NORMAL.
ARE YOU READY TO GO, SLEEPYHEAD?
YOU DON'T WANT TO BE LATE FOR THE RENAISSANCE FESTIVAL!
YOU MEAN IT HASN'T HAPPENED YET, AND A GIANT MONSTER ISN'T RUINING THE FESTIVAL?
HA! HA! HA!
OH, ALEX. YOU HAVE ONE CRAZY IMAGINATION. YOU MUST GET IT FROM YOUR DAD.

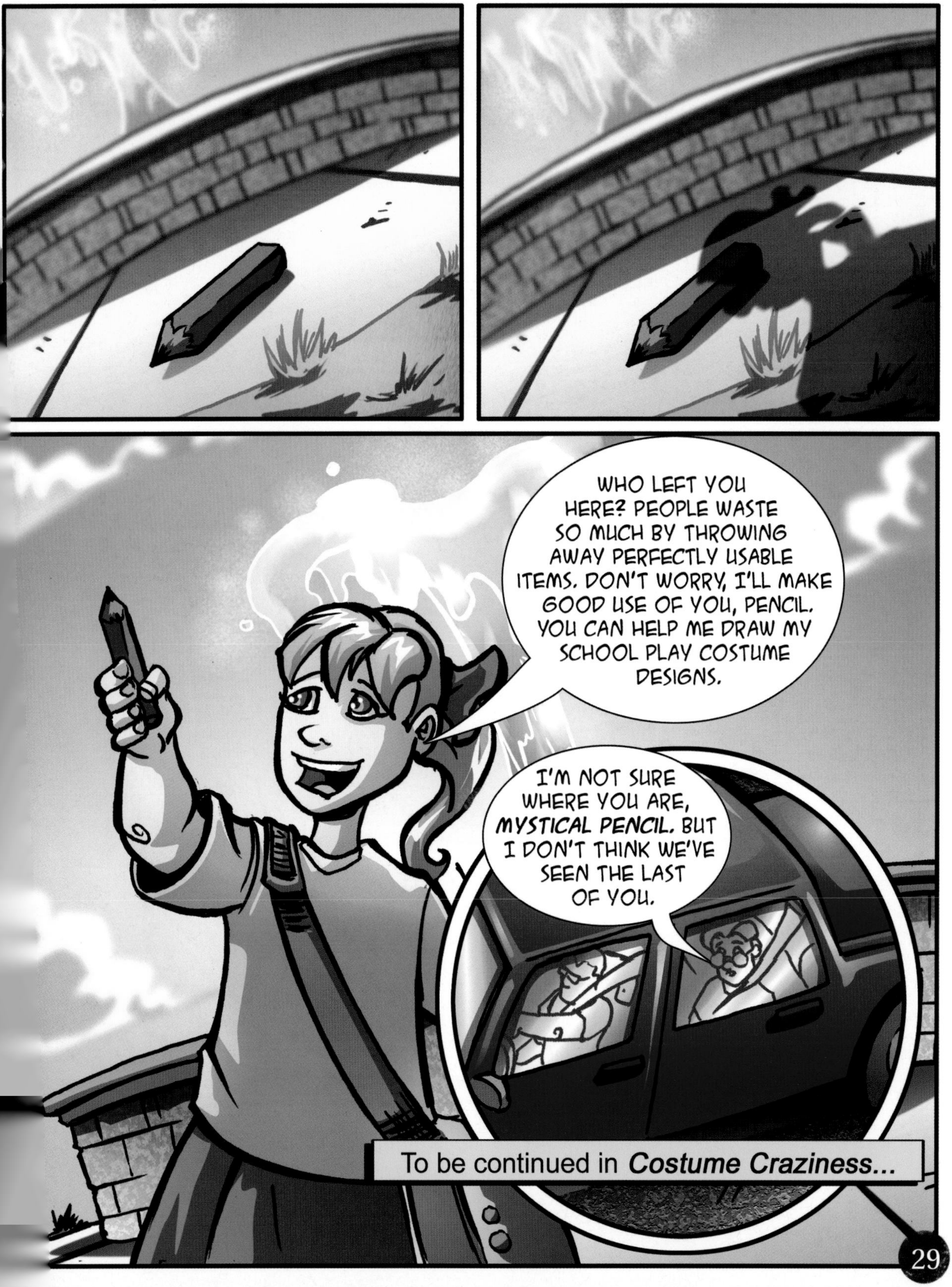
WHO LEFT YOU HERE? PEOPLE WASTE SO MUCH BY THROWING AWAY PERFECTLY USABLE ITEMS. DON'T WORRY, I'LL MAKE GOOD USE OF YOU, PENCIL. YOU CAN HELP ME DRAW MY SCHOOL PLAY COSTUME DESIGNS.
I'M NOT SURE WHERE YOU ARE, *MYSTICAL PENCIL*. BUT I DON'T THINK WE'VE SEEN THE LAST OF YOU.
To be continued in ***Costume Craziness...***

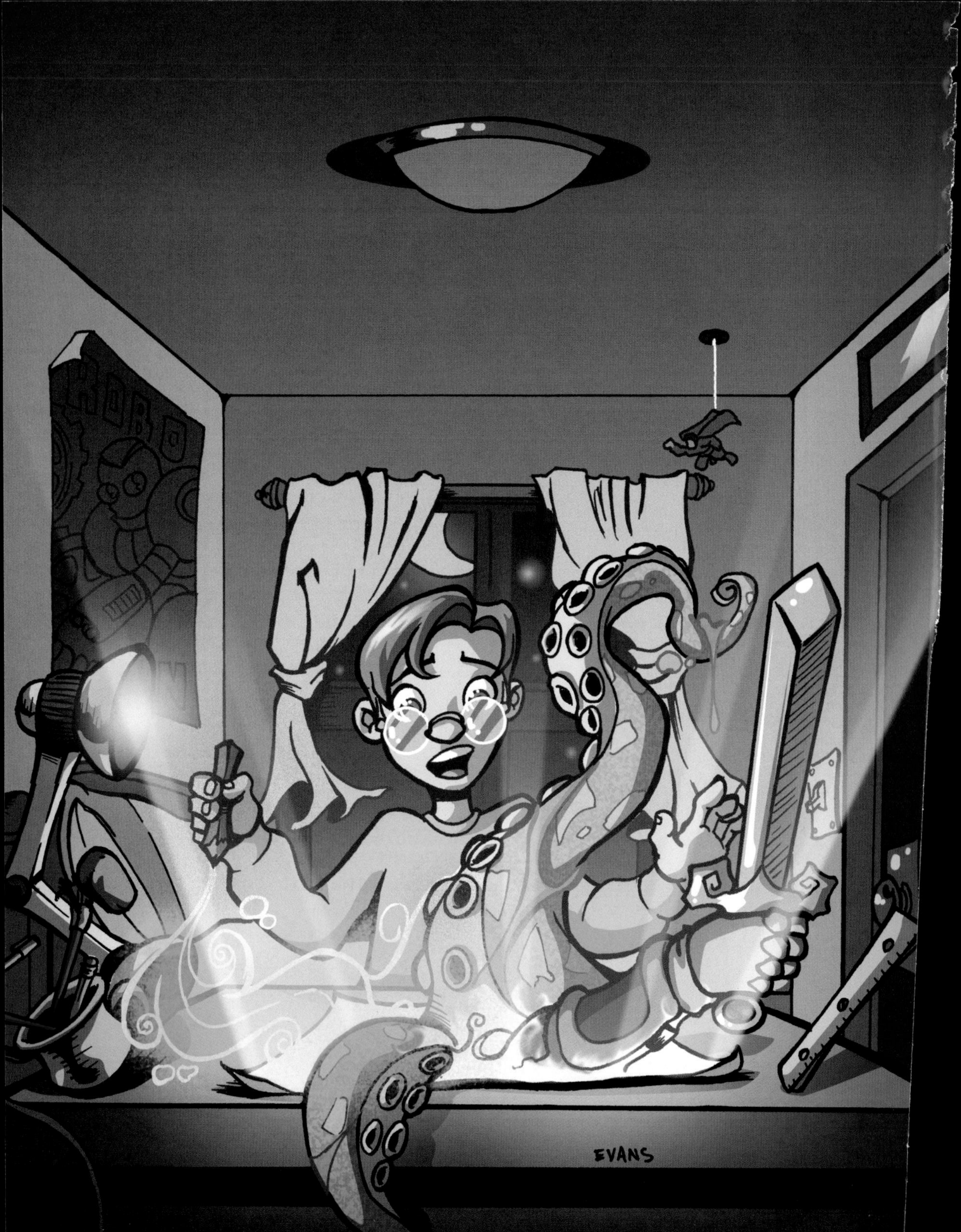
EVANS

How to Draw a Knight!

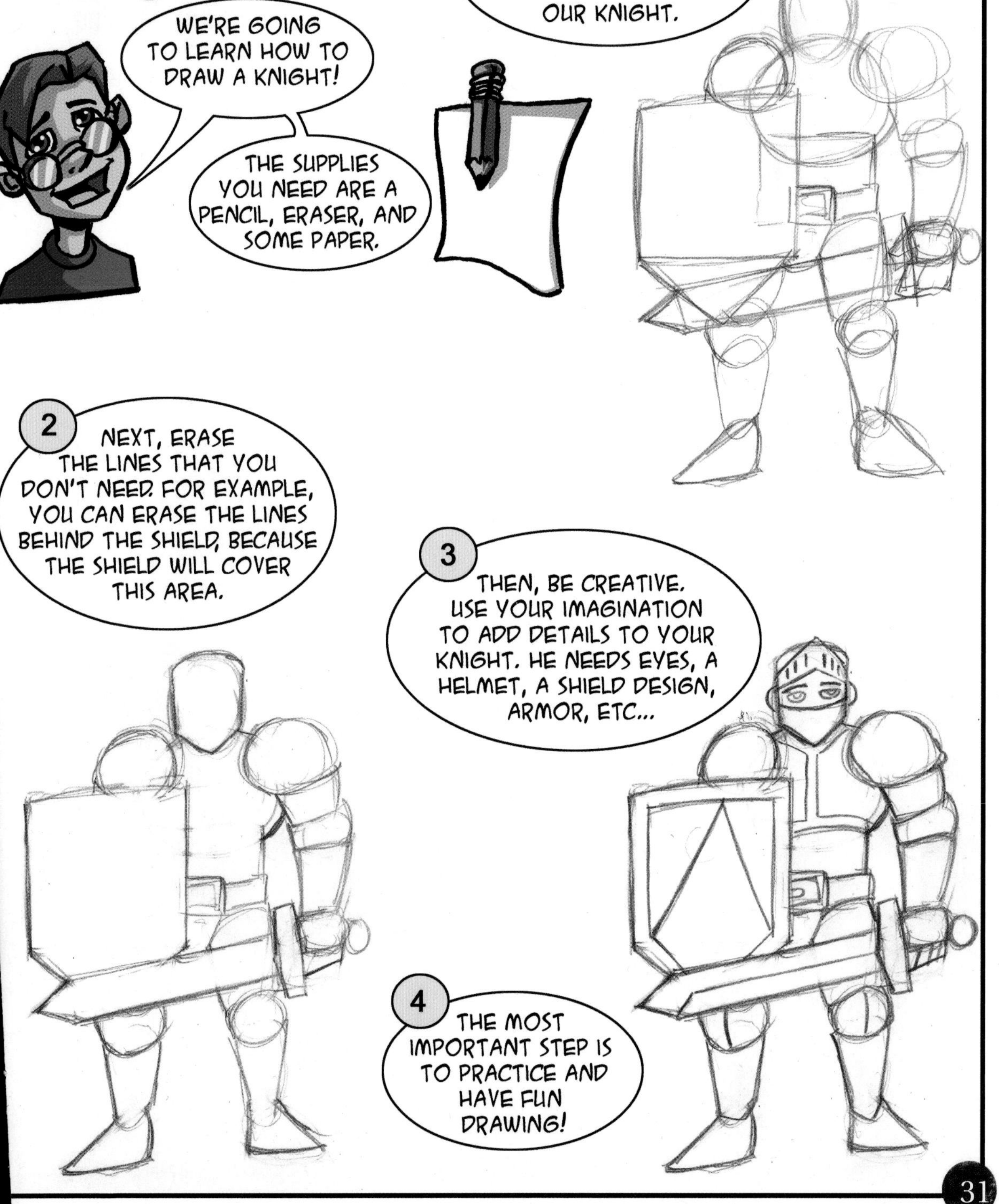
WE'RE GOING TO LEARN HOW TO DRAW A KNIGHT!
THE SUPPLIES YOU NEED ARE A PENCIL, ERASER, AND SOME PAPER.
1
START BY USING BASIC SHAPES LIKE CIRCLES AND SQUARES TO MAKE THE SHAPE OF OUR KNIGHT.
2
NEXT, ERASE THE LINES THAT YOU DON'T NEED. FOR EXAMPLE, YOU CAN ERASE THE LINES BEHIND THE SHIELD, BECAUSE THE SHIELD WILL COVER THIS AREA.
3
THEN, BE CREATIVE. USE YOUR IMAGINATION TO ADD DETAILS TO YOUR KNIGHT. HE NEEDS EYES, A HELMET, A SHIELD DESIGN, ARMOR, ETC...
4
THE MOST IMPORTANT STEP IS TO PRACTICE AND HAVE FUN DRAWING!

About the Author

Dustin Evans was born and raised in Oklahoma. In 2005, Dustin graduated from Oklahoma State University with a BFA in Graphic Design & Illustration. He has since gone on to work with such companies as Disney, IDW Publishing, Magic Wagon, and more. His work can be seen in comic books and children's books and on apparel and TV. He enjoys spending time with his family and pets, reading, drawing, and going to museums and movies.

Dustin begins each page with simple pencil and paper. Working from the script, he creates a rough layout for each page. Once the layouts are ready, he then scans the images into the computer to make them larger. The next step is to print out the larger layout, transfer it to the final page using a light box, and then ink the final image. Dustin then goes back to the computer to scan the final, inked image. Now it's time to add digital color, special effects, and lettering using computer programs. Finally, the image is complete and ready for print after some fine-tuning with any needed edits.

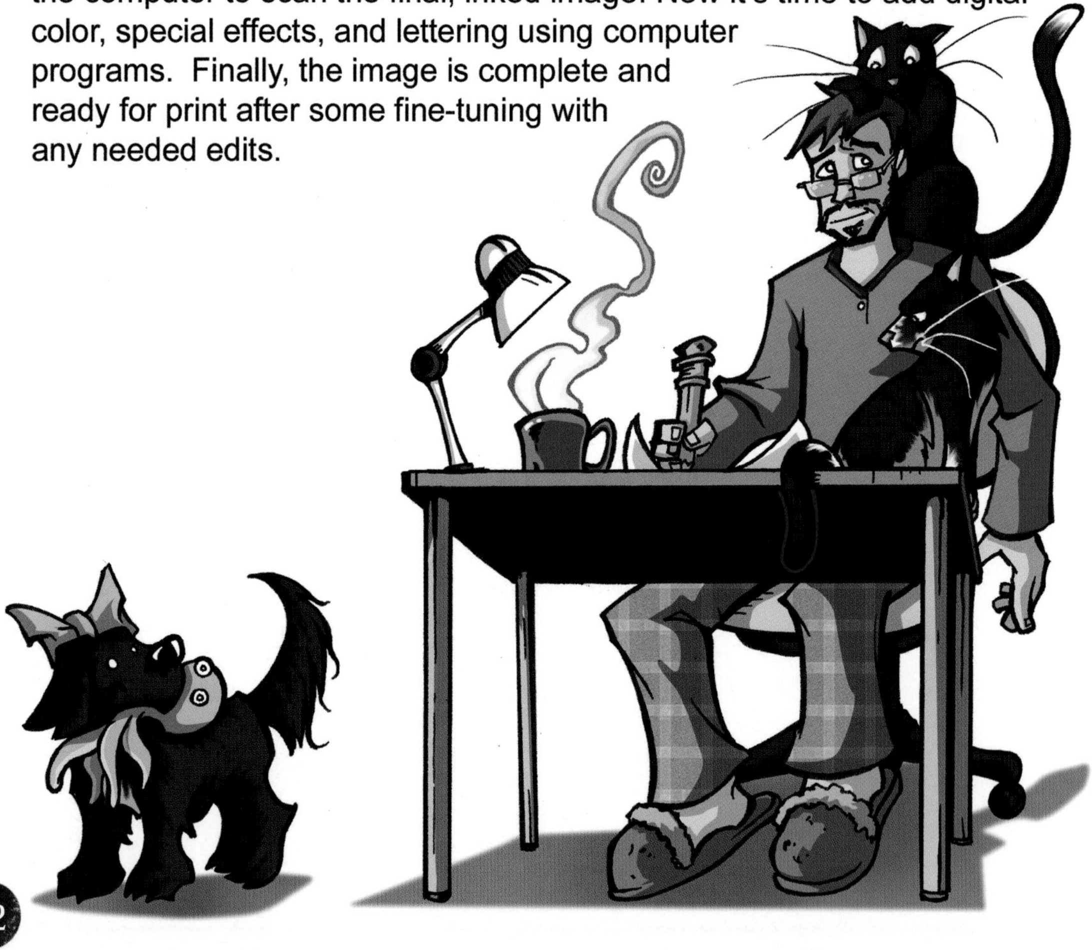